LEADING LADY

Shalamar Parrish

ISBN 978-1-953223-80-7 (paperback)
ISBN 978-1-953223-79-1 (digital)

Rushmore Press LLC
1 800 460 9188
www.rushmorepress.com

Printed in the United States of America

This book is dedicated to my grandmother Norma Jean
Robinson and to my biological mother Edith Robinson-Burns.

May the words that are written in this book cause
you both to smile. I wish that I could come to
heaven and give you both a hug and kiss.

Thank God! Ladies, we did it!

ACKNOWLEDGEMENT

GOD HAS TAUGHT ME a thing or two, about the importance of being grateful. He showed me that humility can take you a long way if ever you remain humble. Thanks so much to the Creator of all things, in heaven and on earth.

Jehovah. Thanks for giving me an opportunity to breathe, your breath of life. Thanks for blessing me with your awesome gift called life. I want nothing more than to achieve your purpose for taking the time to mold me.

To my mother standing in the gap, Terri Daniel. I thank you for taking me in and calling me your own. Through the good and the bad, you have stood by me. I hope that your fears and tears can finally subside. It may have taken a while to see the results from your hard work teaching me the right way to go, but I was listening. I love and thank God for you.

To my prayer warrior, Ms. Johnnie Daniels, Thanks for being the greatest foster mother that any child would be blessed to know. Thanks for still being there for me. Thanks for all you do for children in dayton, ohio. Thanks for your unconditional love. I thank God for you.

To my father Sherman Wheeler and my stepfather James Burns, thanks to you both for loving me.

To my son, Shy'ire, thanks for allowing me to become your adoptive Mother. I promise that I will always cherish my role as your mom. To my grandson Shy'ire jr. You have come into this world and stole my heart!

My other loves Marcus, Jody and Nay'seer. Nothing on this earth will ever take the love away that I have in my mind, heart and soul for each of you. I pray that you each know that I wanted nothing more than to always be able to love, encourage, protect and provide for each of you until I no longer had breath in my body. I will always regret that I couldn't adopt you…

To my God children, God mom loves each of you!

To my brothers and sisters, I can only hope that you all know how important each of you are to my heart. I cherish you all dearly.

To my nieces and nephews, auntie loves each and everyone of you!

To my right and left hands, Arnetta (Peachie) Gary and Kathy Dunson. I could never thank you ladies enough for all you both have done for me, my whole life. You both have been more than my aunts. Thanks for waking up for my late night phone calls. Thanks for telling me when I am wrong though I wanted to hear that I was right! Thanks for being there through it all.

To all my other aunts, Fee, Shirley, Donna and my angel in heaven aunt Tammy… I love you ladies!

To Lillian Ragland, I love you cousin, you have been with me through the thick and the thin. Even an disagreement or two couldn't destroy our bond!

To all my other cousins, including all my cousins who are now resting in heaven. I love each of you so much.

To the rest of my beloved family including the Howe family, May you each know that I love you. May you each remember that I pray for you. Thanks for all your love and support.

To Jose (North) Estermera, Thanks for being my friend and mentor.

To my Columbus, Ohio family, you all are my family for life. You all were there from the beginning.

To my Kentucky family… I love each and everyone of you.

To all parentless children, may each one of you know that you were created to be a gift for God. Hold your head high. Make our Father in Heaven proud!

To everyone touching this novel, may you know that God always loves, protects and provides for you.

To my cousins Travis Jr., Thomas Jr., and little Moni… Our family hasn't been the same since all three of you left us.

To my son, Tyreese Jr. Mommy loves you so much. This world wasn't pure enough for you to be able to live here with your father and myself. You are truly our Angel.

To my Rushmore Publishing thanks for taking me to the next level. Your company has been a pleasure to work with.

To Khloe, thanks for being my awesome go to! You are very important to me.

To my editor and friend Aliza Sollins, I could never thank you enough. You are truly a gift from God.

To my BTW Marketing team, thanks for all you have done and thanks in advance for all you are making become possible for me.

Thanks again!

To my deceased husband, Michael, I miss you so much, I appreciate the time God allowed me to have with you. You showed me that not separation nor death could affect the gift of real love. I will always love you here on earth and in heaven. I'll see you when I get there.

PROLOGUE

Marie beamed as she gave herself a once-over in the mirror. She couldn't help but overhear the news say that Dayton was considered a baby Detroit because of all the crime. She knew all too well that her neighborhood was no stranger to crime, mainly because it was a neighborhood with plenty of single-parent families.

Marie is ready to step up, show off, and get hers. Though twenty might be young in the green-pastured suburbs of Ohio, the streets of Dayton have raised Marie. With two young babies and her sisters to support, Marie has learned how to hustle with what she knows best.

Men are to be used as a protector and a provider. With her beauty, style, and a juiciness that men crave after the first taste—she can pull in a hundred dollars in less than five minutes and have access to some of the neighborhood's most powerful men.

Will her path to become a talented leading lady lead her and her family to a better life? Or are the stakes of this dangerous game too high?

Will her daughter, Harmony, end up following in her footsteps?

Marie

Aᴛ ʟᴇᴀsᴛ ᴛʜᴀᴛ ᴡᴀs what Channel 7 News seemed to believe. Marie just felt like it was a magnet for anyone who loved living on the wrong side of the law—mainly because they had to live the life of crime to make ends meet.

She didn't think the high death rate was a joking matter, but when they said that more drugs were flooding the west side of Dayton, that part made her gleam. She figured the more drugs, the more money. That's the only reason why she even cared to listen. She was fully aware that the streets' revenue had its own stock market. She also knew that the more they made from dealing, the more they'd spend. She already had a substantial amount of drug dealers on her payroll but felt there was always room for one more.

Prostitution was at an all-time high in the city. The oldest profession in history was still a hidden path to wealth in America. Marie took that hard road. She learned all too well how to carry herself like a leading lady. She worked her way into being what most pimps called their main worker or bottom bitch.

This was not her first choice when it came to being a young woman with big dreams, but she knew her chance of becoming a nurse was a little far-fetched when she and her sisters had to make some money now.

Folks outside of Dayton might be surprised at Marie and her sisters' line of work at such a young age; but Marie knew more about sex, love, and hustling at twenty years old than most of those green-pastured, suburban girls would learn in a lifetime. Though she wasn't an adult in the eyes of the law, learning to support her family, her son Lil' Man, and her baby daughter Starla had made her into a woman. She knew how to drive business and get what she needed, however she could.

Back then, it was nothing for a boyfriend to be a woman's protector, provider, and pimp. Marie was always on the lookout for a good man, but she never wanted a pimp. She just didn't like the thought of giving a man half the proceeds of her hard day's work. She had too many mouths to feed already.

Marie continued getting herself ready but was interrupted when her mother, Nancy, came in the front door.

"Marie…Shell…Stacy…Tracy! Who's home?"

"Me, Momma. I'm in the bathroom," called Marie.

Nancy came up on Marie as she was putting on her makeup in the bathroom.

"I need for you to stay home with your kids, Marie. Quit leaving them off on Shell."

"Okay, Momma, but I got to hustle. We got my kids' needs and your kids' needs. Your income is not enough for all of us." Marie leaned in toward the mirror and drew on a thick line of eyeliner.

"You heard what I said," Nancy gave her orders from the doorway.

"Yes, ma'am."

Marie knew whatever Nancy said was law. She and her sisters had much respect for their mom, no matter what, much fear and respect. She thought twice about making her decision to go out with Harold that night.

But in the end, she knew what she was going to do. Her date was going to happen, whether Nancy liked it or not.

One street was her favorite for shopping, for clothes, men, and whatever else she wanted. Gettysburg Avenue was the most popular strip for those who wanted to drive down and see all they could see and be all they could be. It was a beautiful spring afternoon. The sun was shining, school was out on break, and the streets were popping.

Marie called up her girl Butter to see if she wanted to get out of the house and *see and be seen.* They never let lack of a car stop them from visiting that privileged street. Walking was always more fun anyway.

Marie was a beautiful girl. She was blessed with dark skin that felt like silk. Her eyes were the color of almonds, and her lips were full. She stood at five feet nine inches with the shape of a goddess. Her daughter, Harmony, would later be graced with a beauty of her own.

Marie chose the women with whom she ran wisely and had to have a group of them who were bad. They had to look right, act right, and get plenty of money. Butter had been her girl since grade school.

They had kept each other's secrets and traded guys, clothes, and favors since day one. True to her name, Butter had skin with a golden glow and thick curves that men always told her looked good enough to eat. Together, the two of them together usually got what they wanted and then some.

They met on the corner to begin their walk.

"Girl, I am so glad you called me," said Butter. "I was about to go crazy stuck up in that house. Where you trying to walk?"

"Anywhere, girl. Long as we find some fine brothers and go shopping along the way."

Walking down Gettysburg, Marie and Butter swayed their hips like lionesses on the prowl. A trumpeting of horns and shouts of praise surrounded them as they began their mission. Marie loved days like this when the weather was fine and people were out. She took note of everyone she passed, what new fashion trends were good, what bars were hot, and who drove what type of car. She looked out from beneath her famously long eyelashes and took it all in.

They stuck to their usual plan to stop at a street corner by a stoplight. They knew that they would get more attention since men driving by would have to stop, wait, and observe who was passing by.

They stopped at an intersection to admire the latest trends in the window of a clothing store. The clothes were cute, so they decided to go inside and shop around a while before turning around and starting for home. As they walked inside, Marie started telling Butter about an incident that occurred between her and one of her tricks.

"Butter, you should have seen this fool when his wife walked in!" Marie started. "Turns out she had followed him right to the hotel room. Caught him with his pants down and his money out and everything. His dick melted so fast, I thought it would drop off!"

"Damn, girl!" Butter laughed. "I had that happen to me too once! I hope you got that money though."

"Of course, girl!" Marie waved her hand. "I snatched that money while she was hitting him. I got the hell out of there!"

They were still laughing when they got to the door.

From behind the counter, a tall, lean man watched them enter. His skin was the color of new leather, tan and polished.

"Hello, ladies," he purred. "May I learn the reason why you both have entered my presence and establishment with those beautiful smiles and cheerful hearts?"

Marie answered first. "Oh, sorry, we were just discussing something that happened the other day."

She and Butter exchanged knowing looks.

"Well, please share," he replied, leaning in toward both beauties.

They looked at each other and then at him.

"We can't," they replied in unison.

"Well, how about I help you find an outfit?" he asked, trying a different path to continue the conversation.

"We're just looking," they said.

"Certainly, certainly," he replied.

As Marie browsed the racks, Butter decided she wanted to flirt. She tried on every necklace hanging on display in front of the store, making sure her reflection in the mirror showed to Mr. Handsome behind the counter.

She tugged down her dress to make sure there was as much cleavage as possible. The rhinestones gleamed to show off the gifts God had given her.

Marie decided to let her friend have her fun. But when Butter turned to look through a rack of low-cut tops, Marie felt the man staring in her direction. She looked up slowly. The man looked Marie up and down and gave her a wink.

Marie was never the type who chased a man—she chased money. That winking was going to help her pay no bills, so she ignored his gestures and allowed Butter to continue her quest.

Suddenly, the perfect outfit appeared before her. A blue-jean-and-red bell-bottom jumpsuit, which she knew would fit every curve of her body and make her dark skin shine.

"Excuse me, may I try this on?" she asked, batting her lashes and finally returning the winks of the man behind the counter.

"Sure. The fitting room is back there." He smiled back at her, waving his arm as if throwing a rose to his queen.

"Do you need my help?" he asked.

"No, thank you." Marie quickly walked to the back of the room, switching her hips back and forth with each step. She could feel his eyes following each move she made.

At the dressing room, she reached down and stroked the fabric of the beautiful garments that would soon be hers.

Marie pasted that outfit on. It showed off every curve possible for a woman to possess. As she stared at herself in the mirror, a smile crept across her face. She knew that with this outfit on, she wouldn't have to say a word. It would speak for her.

Marie strutted out of the fitting room as if she were a Fifth Avenue fashion model. Imaginary cameras flashed to take her picture, and invisible crowds applauded her arrival. But Marie only had the attention of one man on her mind.

As she strode into the middle of the store, she twirled around to show off the front and back, stroking her hands over her splendid curves, showing off that perfect outfit. The man behind the counter couldn't look away. His mouth dropped.

"Gorgeous! Don't hurt me," he moaned. "Baby, you are simply wearing that outfit." He couldn't stop calling out his praise.

"Damn...Gorgeous."

The other customers in the store had also turned to stare.

"Baby, can I please get your number so I can call and thank your momma?" asked an older man pawing through a selection of socks.

Other customers around the store laughed, and someone gave a low whistle.

Marie had schooled all the with whom chicks she ran about the rules of the game. She told them that men were nothing more than human dogs with money. They only liked to chase and not get caught, so she argued they should play them like they should be played.

The whole purpose for their walk was to get chosen, and now it was paying off.

"So I take it that you like the outfit?" Marie asked.

"Not as much as I like you in the outfit," he said.

Marie raised her eyebrows and gave the man behind the counter a long look. She turned and strode back toward the dressing room. She changed into her clothes, then returned with the jumpsuit draped over her arm.

Butter had realized this round was Marie's and was outside smoking a cigarette. She leaned against the light pole, checking out any nice cars that rolled by. Marie waved and held up her hand to let her know she would be a minute.

As Marie approached the counter, the man decided to formally introduce himself.

"Hi"—he put out his hand to grasp hers, staring deeply into her almond eyes—"name's Harold. I'm the owner of the store."

Owner, Marie thought. She liked the sound of that.

"Hello, Harold, I'm Marie. It's nice to meet you." She returned his gaze and smiled.

"No, let me be the first to say that the pleasure is all mine." He bent down to kiss her hand, his eyes sweeping along the length of her body.

She placed the beautiful new outfit on the counter.

"Hey, Gorgeous, how about this?" He leaned in toward her. "How about I'll let you walk out of my store with that outfit for free, if you would do me the honor of letting me see you later tonight in it."

"So you're saying that you would like for me to model for you?" Marie responded, smiling to herself.

"Yes, but that's only if I can take you out and show you off to some of my close friends. With all that beauty, I would be a fool to keep you locked behind closed doors all to myself."

Marie was flattered. "Well, Harold, in that case, I shall see you around nine?"

"Gorgeous, nine is perfect."

She took the outfit, he took the address, and soon they would be making history, with Harmony included.

2

"Headquarters" was what Marie and her sisters called home.

By the time she and Butter returned to Headquarters from their adventures, it was around six o'clock in the evening. Rushing to get ready for her 9:00 p.m. date, she had to keep her two kids occupied.

"Shell, please get the kids so they can get ready for dinner," she asked.

Her younger sister was washing bottles at the sink.

"No," said Shell, turning to look at Marie. "They are your kids, and they are missing their mother."

As soon as Marie started bringing home babies, Shell was the one who stayed home from school to change diapers so her sister could work. Marie appreciated the help, but sometimes Shell would try to act like she ran the house.

Marie sighed and looked into the sitting room where her babies were playing.

"I know, but I got to work." She went over to pick up her firstborn whom they all called Lil' Man. "Here baby, Mommy misses you." She gave him a kiss on his sticky cheek.

Not wanting to be left out, Starla crawled over toward her mother and banged a rattling butterfly on her leg.

Marie picked her up too and gave them both a hug. "Mommy loves both of you."

Then it was time for business.

"Here, Shell, take this money and put it up." She handed her sister a stack of cash. "That's for the light bill. If Momma asks you if I left any money, tell her no."

"All right," said Shell.

"Have ya'll ate?" asked Marie.

"Yeah, a little," replied Shell.

"Well, take this and walk to the grocery," said Marie, handing her sister another wad of cash.

"How am I going to do that? I got yours and Momma's kids," Shell snapped, giving Marie attitude.

"Shell, stop it!" yelled Marie. "You chose to stay here with them because you like the money I give you. I'm out busting my ass while you're here watching cartoons!"

"Whatever, like I said." Shell rolled her eyes.

"No, like *I* said." Marie's word won. "You can go while I am still home. Catch a cab so you can get there and get back before I leave. I got somewhere to be at nine."

As Shell collected the kids and started putting them in the stroller, Marie asked, "Where is Tracy and Stacy?"

"Girl, they both have been in and out of here, bringing money home. They asked where you were because they have some work for all of you to do."

"For real?" asked Marie. "When?"

"Tonight, I guess."

"Well, if it's nothing major, then I am going to have to sit this one out."

"Why, Marie? We need all the money we can get."

"Girl, hush, don't ever talk to me like that," said Marie. "I know what I'm doing."

Though she loved her mother for raising her and her sisters to keep their heads high, their house clean, and watch each other's backs, Marie would be breaking Nancy's orders tonight. It was time to become her own woman. She hoped tonight would be the first step toward the life she always wanted, full of glamour, style, and class.

Nine o'clock came so fast! She had just put the kids to sleep. It had taken over an hour to put Lil' Man down. He fought her every step of the way. If she didn't know any better, she would say he knew what she was about to do and he was trying his best to stop her.

There was a slight tap on the door, but before she could reach it, Nancy got to it.

"Who is it?" she asked.

"Harold."

"Harold, who?" Nancy questioned through the worn wood door.

"Oh, Momma, that's for me," sighed Marie.

Marie got her purse and brushed past her mother because she knew Harold would have gotten the third degree.

"Bye, Momma," she said. "I put the kids to sleep. I'll be back soon."

"You better be," said Nancy.

As they approached his yellow Fleetwood, Harold gave her a kiss on the cheek.

"Mmmm," he breathed next to her ear. "Gorgeous, you smell like the Garden of Eden."

When they reached the curb, he stepped out and opened the car door.

She couldn't believe it. Though she had received her fair share of compliments, Harold's words felt like they transformed her into a goddess. She felt magnificent in his eyes.

He leaned past and opened the car door for her, sending a thrill through her body as his hand led her inside.

She smiled and slid in to those buttery Cadillac seats as if she belonged there. As the door clicked gently shut, she realized that it was the first time a man had ever opened a car door for her.

Wow, this man really does know how to treat a lady, she thought. *What are the chances of me lucking up on a man who is fine, gas money, plus knows how to treat a lady? Shoot, all the ones I've encountered lately just got money, so I been settling just for that. This man got class.*

He looked over at her and smiled as they drove along.

"Gorgeous, you really look nice."

"Thanks. You're looking fine yourself," she said, glancing up and down his body shamelessly.

"Is that right?" he flirted.

"Yes, if I must say so myself."

"Thanks, I try," he said.

Truth be told, Harold did more than try. The man would take hours just to get prepared for his workday. He actually had his own beautician. When the average man was getting haircuts or shape-ups, Harold would be at the salon getting his hair, nails, and feet tended to.

He shopped at all the finer stores—Thal's, Metropolitans, Donna Field's, Wikes, and Craig's, just to name a few. There was also Ms. Lucy, his personal seamstress. If the store didn't have it, then she would just have to make it.

Harold was a man who had worn a suit every day since grade school. He knew he was going to be somebody one day. That drive paid off. He was not only one of the biggest drug dealers in Dayton but also one of the biggest pimps.

He took his life and his money seriously. Hands down, he was one of the smartest hustlers in the game. When many of the other kingpins and hustlers were blowing money, he had invested his in a business and saved a great deal.

Now he was riding one of the newest makes that Cadillac offered. He had a rule he lived by, kind of like a soldier's creed—break a bitch's self-esteem, break her pockets, and if she gets out of line, break her back.

Not much was said as they drove, listening to Earth, Wind & Fire playing loudly over the car's stereo system. Marie leaned toward him to get his attention. Turning down his music, he showed her that he wanted to know what was on her mind.

"Yes, Gorgeous?"

"I just wanted to know what our plans were."

"Baby, I am about to take you somewhere real nice and we are about to have the time of our lives," Harold replied, smiling at Marie's innocence.

She was starting to wonder why everything this man said sounded like a riddle or a rhyme.

"Where might that be?" she asked.

"To The Ball," he said.

"The Ball on Third Street?" She couldn't believe it.

The Ball was the most popular club on the west side of Dayton. Anyone winning the game on the street went there. She had often walked past the mysterious red doorway and wondered about getting inside. One day. It looked like today was that day.

"That'll be the one." Harold grinned.

"I can't get in there!"

"Why not?" he asked.

"I'm not old enough," she said shyly, looking at him from under her long lashes.

She had never told him her age. Though she was a mother and a caretaker for her kids and her family, her government ID still said she was only twenty.

Now that she thought about it, she didn't know his age either. It really didn't matter to her because she was thinking about money, and money was more valuable than age.

Harold wasn't worried about it.

"Baby, you're with me," he assured. He gave her a confident smile with those perfect white teeth and winked. "I own that club."

She sat back and took everything in—the music, the conversation, and her future with Harold, the shot caller.

The night was still young, and the action on Gettysburg was just getting started. On the weekend, the parking lot was like a who's who of the street's most important hustlers and their women. A night like tonight would surely bring out a crowd. Marie knew that for certain. By this hour, the sun had finished playing its game of peekaboo, and the wind rushed through the trees with a cool and pleasing breeze.

She knew that it was the time of night when all the players on the street quit working for the day. They would rush home and put on their fly gear and pull out their fancy whips. She was elated watching all of the cars pull in.

Harold had opened his sunroof earlier, and it had caused her wig's curls to shift a little.

She didn't mind because she enjoyed her hair blowing in the wind like white women often had the privilege of experiencing.

She decided to check herself in the mirror. Finishing up, she looked at her beau for approval.

"Baby, you are one sexy woman," he said with all sincerity. "You have the longest eyelashes I have ever seen."

"Thanks," Marie smiled, trying not to betray her heart fluttering with pleasure and excitement.

Before she could get anything else out, their car was flooded by adoring fans. She felt as if she and Harold were superstars, like they were on stage.

"Hitler, man, that's a sweet ride," shouted a brotha with shine beaming from huge rocks in each ear and gold chains to match.

Marie froze. *Did they just call him Hitler?*

She heard the name shouted out again and again by the crowd, "Hitler, Hitler."

Her heart jumped up into her throat. She felt dizzy and out of her head.

Who am I riding with?

She had made a mistake by asking the question out loud, but fuck it, she needed to know.

Harold paused his conversation with a man in a dark suit to answer her question.

"Yes, Gorgeous, that's my street name." He gave her a confident smile and returned to his business conversation.

They were speaking in low voices, and Marie knew from the other man's gigantic build and expensive-looking suit that he was no street-level dealer.

Marie felt her blood pressure rise. *How could I have been so stupid? Is this a setup?*

All at once, she remembered hearing a story about a man named Hitler stealing Butter's stepsister from her husband. The story she heard was that Hitler promised big-time money if she would work for him. She left her husband to try to earn that money but only got deeper and deeper in debt to Hitler. She ended up walking the track, day and night.

Once her husband found out what was going on, he went to go get her back. The husband was still missing to this day. Hitler was the name on the street for the reason why.

Marie started to worry to herself. *This man has a reputation of being bad news. How did I end up here? I have got to get myself up out of this.*

"Excuse me, Harold—I mean, Hitler," she said.

A skinny, dusty man shuffled over and was trying to clean the windshield of the Cadillac with a bucket of soap and crumpled newspaper.

"Ay, man, get away from my car!" Hitler yelled.

The man flinched and ran off.

Then the man known as Hitler turned to Marie to answer her.

"Yes, Gorgeous?"

"I don't know why, but I'm starting to feel sick." She felt the blood rush to her face and fanned herself.

"For real? What's hurting you?"

She was surprised to see him look at her with genuine concern.

"I am getting the worst headache. There is no way that I can go out like this." She pressed a perfectly manicured nail to her forehead in a motion of pain.

"We don't have to go out," he replied. "We can stop by the store. I'll get you what you need. Then we can just go to my apartment and chill."

Here was a man about whom she had only heard horror stories wanting to stop whatever he was trying to do to take care of her. This was so unusual for Marie. She was always the caretaker, but now here was this powerful man offering to drop everything and get what she needed. She was flattered.

There was something else. Truth be told, she was curious to know more about this high roller life. She knew she was no ordinary female. She was no fool. She knew the costs of this life. And right now, she decided she was willing to take that gamble. Maybe tonight was her lottery ticket.

She decided to see where the night led. Maybe it would pay off big. She shook off her fears. It was time to play the game, for real. It was time to get her on the level she deserved. Harold was a big fish, and someone would catch him. She decided she would be that woman.

Taking a long, slow breath, she looked into the side-view mirror and smoothed down her hair, erasing all traces of worry from her face.

Harold got back in the car and shut out the noise from the crowd outside. He leaned forward and turned the music on low. Marie felt like they were in their own private bubble, upholstered in soft leather and full of the scent of good cologne.

They rested for a moment, listening to the music. Harold turned to look at Marie.

She waited to see what his move would be. Her heart began to race as he slowly reached over toward her. She stayed absolutely still as his warm hand brushed her cheek.

He moved his fingers up to trace gently along her ear, rubbing and tugging it where she was most sensitive. Pleasure lit up her body, erasing any fears. All she could think about was his tongue and how good it would feel being licked and teased by it. This clearly was a man who knew how to touch a woman.

Suddenly, Harold let go of her, resting his hands on the steering wheel. He looked over at her and smiled.

"I think I might know what will help you feel better, Gorgeous. I've got some high-quality goody powder for you to try. I'll bet you've never had anything like it before."

Marie agreed. She had never had anything like that before, but she couldn't wait to try.

They lined up several on a small mirror between the seats. Harold handed her a rolled-up hundred-dollar bill. As Marie leaned over to do her first line, she caught a glimpse of her reflection in the mirror.

Hey there, Gorgeous, she thought. *Welcome to the big time.*

Strolling up to the front door of the club and having two men open both their doors was an honor. They were treated like royalty.

"Mr. Hitler, who is that beautiful lady you got with you tonight?"

"This is my leading lady."

Marie loved the sound of that.

Leading lady—how clever, she thought. *How descriptive.*

She had always thought of herself as a worthy leading lady. Now one of the most famous brothas in Dayton knew it too.

Yes, he had a terrifying street name. But so did every other brotha in this club. And this one owned the club.

As they swept into the crowded room, Marie felt like his equal, like together they owned everything before them. Marie kept her arm intertwined with his as they glided past the bar. Everything was decorated with style and class, from the top-shelf liquor lit from behind to the well-dressed customers wearing their best and boldest outfits.

She felt looks coming from a group of females clustered by the bar and heard one of them say loudly, "No, he didn't bring that young-ass girl here!"

Marie looked in her direction to let her know that she had heard the insult. She then smiled and wrapped her arm around her man even tighter.

They came to a halt when they reached a section with leather couches and cranberry and gold accents to match. They sat on a gold leather couch that was centered in the middle, so they could see out on to the dance floor. Sitting on it felt like she was floating on a cloud.

"Why is this room set up like this?" she asked.

"This is a room for the VIP—very important people," he said, winking at her.

He took off his jacket and leaned back on the couch with his arms spread wide.

A man in a black suit came over to their table.

"How are you this evening, sir? May I get you and your guest something to drink?"

"A bottle of Crown." He turned toward Marie. "Gorgeous, do you drink?"

"Yes." She sure did.

"All right then. We'll drink that Crown and smoke this joint."

It sounded like a beautiful way to start off the evening.

Truth be told, Marie did drink and smoke but never Crown. That was top of the line. She had heard about Crown Royal, but her drink of choice was MD 20/20. That Pineapple Red was more for a lady, so that became her favorite. As soon as she had her first sip of Crown, she swore she would never take another sip of anything less.

Marie enjoyed every moment of sweet drinks and the thump of the bass as her man held her on the dance floor, whispering sensual lyrics into her ear. She leaned into him, swaying to the beat. His large hands slid down and covered the curve of her behind. His touch felt amazing, mixed with the high of the night. She pressed in closer to him, sliding her bare thighs against the fine fabric of his beautiful suit. Her body shook to the music, and she smiled.

The club closed at three, and it was definitely past time for Marie to get home. She knew Nancy would be pissed if she came home that late. Nancy's philosophy was, "Don't come home if you can't come at a decent hour."

Marie knew that three wasn't a decent hour. But spending the night with a man and not getting paid was a bigger sin in her book, so she decided to face Nancy instead.

Sitting in front of their apartment building, she told Harold how she had enjoyed being with him.

"It was a pleasure being in your presence as well, Gorgeous," said Harold.

He reached over and caught her mouth in his with a long, slow kiss. The tip of his tongue softly flicked in and out, caressing her parted lips, and Marie fought the urge to lean in and grab it with her teeth. Harold opened his eyes slowly to look at her.

"I hope you will allow me to see you later on today."

Marie smiled. She truly felt like a leading lady.

"Why, of course," she replied before grabbing her purse and slipping out of the car.

She could feel him watching her as she crept quietly to Nancy's front door.

As she turned her key to sneak inside, she could hear Harold driving off. The coast was clear. All were sleeping, and soon she would be too.

She was able to quietly make it into the bedroom she shared with her twin older sisters, Tracy and Stacy. It was an art knowing how to take off her high heels, bracelets, purse, or anything that could click or jingle or bang in the night, revealing to Nancy that rules had been broken.

Of course, she should have known that there was no hiding anything from her sisters. As soon as the bedroom door clicked behind her, the lamp was on, and Stacy and Tracy were up in, bed waiting to drag every bit of news out of her.

"Sista, where were you tonight?" asked Stacy.

"You missed out!" said Tracy. "We made 150! It was a group of corner boys that had a big payday, not even some old nasty men either. They were cute and even had some of that good stuff for us. We told Shell to tell you we had a job. Where were you?"

Marie couldn't stop the dreamy smile from spreading across her face.

"Girls, I had a ball myself."

"How much did you get?" Stacy went right to the point.

The older sisters always asked Marie what she made, bracing themselves for her total because she always brought home more than they both did.

Marie took off her wig and laid it on the dresser, then moved to the mirror to start removing her makeup.

"Calm down, ladies, it wasn't that type of night."

She opened a jar of cold cream and dabbed at her eyes to take off the mascara.

"What do you mean then?" asked Tracy. "That must be some kind of man for you to go out on a date and not get paid!"

Marie looked up at her sisters in the mirror.

"Yes, he is some kind of man," she said. "I met him when Butter and I were shopping on Gettysburg. He bought me a beautiful outfit and asked me out to The Ball! We drove there in his Cadillac and were treated like royalty. All the best drinks and seats in the VIP section. Turns out, he is the owner of the club!"

The twins looked at each other, and then smiled at Marie.

"Wow, girl, that sounds nice!" said Tracy. "What's his name?"

"Well..." Marie suddenly seemed very busy removing the last traces of lipstick. It took her a moment to respond. "His name is Harold."

"Never heard of him," said Stacy.

Tracy was quick to jump in. "Girl, you know a playa driving a Caddy and owning a club don't go by no 'Harold.'" She turned to Marie. "What's his street name?"

"Ummm..." Marie took her time picking out a bandanna to wrap around her hair. "Actually, I think Butter might know him. But she didn't recognize him when we met him at his store. You know how sometimes you hear someone's name on the street...it's hard to know how much you hear on the street is true."

"I know that's right," said Tracy. "Everybody out there on the corner can talk."

"So how does Butter know him then?" said Stacy.

Marie knew she would have to tell them sooner or later. There was no hiding anything from her sisters, and everybody would be talking by tomorrow morning about how they saw her at The Ball. Her sisters would know the truth soon enough.

"Well," said Marie, "you remember when Butter's stepsister went to work for that dude—"

"Hitler!" the twins interrupted before she could get the rest of her sentence out.

"Right," she said.

"What did you do?" asked Stacy.

"Are you crazy?" asked Tracy.

"Shhhhh!" Marie hushed them before her sisters' surprised shouts woke up Nancy and got them all in trouble. "It's not what you think. Harold was the most real man I have ever been with."

"He treated you right?" Tracy got that same defensive tone she always took when she was worried about her sisters.

"Yes!" said Marie. "From the moment we met, he has treated me like royalty. Like I said, we met at his shop on Gettysburg, and he gave me the gift of this beautiful outfit."

She picked up the new bell-bottom jumpsuit from the back of the chair and smoothed out the wrinkles before hanging it up in the closet.

"You can tell he takes care of himself. He always looks fresh and dressed to all get out. Being with him at that club tonight was like being with a movie star. Everyone knows him and treats him with respect. He calls me Gorgeous, and he is the first man who ever opened a door for me or bought me drinks without trying to get me in bed."

"He opened your door for you?" asked Stacy.

"Yes, girl!" said Marie, excited.

"He didn't try to have sex?" questioned Stacy.

"Nope." Marie slipped on a silky nightgown and tucked herself into the sheets on the other bed in the room.

Tracy and Stacy shared a bed on the other side of the room. They were both sitting up in bed to get all the news they could on this new development.

"He wants to see you again?" asked Stacy.

"Yes!" Marie couldn't stop the smile from spreading across her face.

"Well, sis, I just want you to be careful," sighed Tracy. She and Stacy looked at each other, and then back at Marie. "Please keep us informed with all the details about him. Just in case, we have to pay somebody to kill him."

"You know I will." Marie smiled at her sister's over-the-top offer to protect her. Tracy was always dramatic. "I appreciate your concern, but you know I can take care of myself. This isn't my first time around the block. And I think I have found a good one this time."

She knew her sisters were worried, but Marie believed you had to take risks if you wanted to make it to the big time. Later on, she could check in with Butter to find out more about Harold's past, just to make sure.

You never know if the stories on the street are true anyway, she thought. *This guy named Hitler might be rough, but it might just be corner gossip.*

For now, she just wanted to enjoy the glow of one of the most exciting nights of her life.

"Okay, girl," said Tracy. "Just keep us in the know. Good night."

"Good night," answered Marie.

She cut out the lamp between their beds. Then she drifted off to sleep, dreaming of bright lights, sweet drinks, and the smell of good cologne filling the plush interior of a canary-yellow Cadillac.

$$\text{———}\ \maltese\ 4\ \maltese\ \text{———}$$

Around nine thirty the next morning, she woke up hungry. Tracy and Stacy were gone, and she could hear Shell out in the living room playing with Lil' Man and Starla. She put on her robe and went to the kitchen to make breakfast. Before she could get her bacon out, she received a page.

She checked the pager with an annoyed look.

"Dammit, how am I going to see who this is at this time of morning?" she thought out loud. "We have to get a telephone. I am about sick of having to use Ms. Lee's phone. I am tired of paying her fifty cents per call, then having to give her some of Momma's cigarettes for free. I've had it with that old hag!"

She decided this call would just have to wait. She opened the fridge to get breakfast together.

By 11:00 a.m. she, Shell, and the kids were fed and dressed. She then decided that she'd go to the corner phone booth to call the number that had paged her earlier. As she dialed, she was hoping that that was about money because she had promised her sisters that she would take them to do some summer shopping.

Someone on the other end picked up.

"Hello, did someone call a pager?" asked Marie.

"Only if it belongs, to a gorgeous woman."

Marie's heart jumped as the low voice of her new man came across the line. She took a long, quiet breath and smiled into the phone.

"Well, good morning to you, handsome."

"Did you dream about me?"

Marie was good at this game. She gave a flirtatious laugh and replied with pleasure, "You certainly showed me a wonderful time last night."

"I enjoyed treating you like the princess you are, Gorgeous."

Marie was thrilled.

"You had the attention of everyone in the club, baby girl," Harold continued. "It was a pleasure watching you light up the room with your beauty and class. One night of dancing with you was not enough for me. I would love to take you out again sometime. Are you interested in getting to know me better?"

Marie twirled the cord from the phone around her finger.

"I think that could be arranged. What do you have in mind?"

"I have brunch every Sunday at the Crown Plaza Hotel. Would you join me?"

"I would love to," said Marie. "Brunch would be fabulous."

"Wonderful," said Harold. "I'll pick you up tomorrow at eleven."

Marie hung up the phone. Her cheeks felt hot with excitement, mixed with some nerves. So what if she did not know what *brunch* meant? She was going to the Crown Plaza with a handsome, classy man. She would figure out what to do at a brunch someway. She knew that she had to ask somebody what it was so that she could dress accordingly.

She thought carefully and decided to ask Nancy. She'd do it in a way to make her mother think that she was just interested in finding out what the word meant. Well, she really did need to know what the word meant!

She found her mother washing dishes at the sink when she got home.

"Hey, Momma," said Marie. "I was just out returning some pages."

"Mmmm," Nancy was only half listening as she scrubbed at the plates like they had wronged her.

A clean home was everything to her. Her family might not live in the best neighborhood or have the fanciest clothes or furniture, but what they did have was spic and span and sparkling clean.

Marie poured herself a cup of coffee and tried to act casual. "I might go out later and hang with Butter. She's got some new magazines that have some real cute fashion tips."

"Okay, Marie, but don't be over there too late. You know you got Lil' Man and Starla to take care of later," answered Nancy as she rinsed out some jelly jars.

"I know, I know," said Marie, sipping coffee. "So…if someone were going to a brunch, what do you think they would wear?"

Nancy looked up from the dishes. "Why, who is going to brunch?"

"Momma, nobody. I was just trying to figure out what the word meant." Marie played innocent. "We were looking at magazines, and they were talking about brunch in it."

"It's exactly what it sounds like, girl," answered Nancy as she picked up the sponge again. "Breakfast and lunch together—eggs, and hash browns, and waffles, and all that."

"That's what I thought," said Marie. "I was just curious."

Marie settled on a colorful sundress with strappy sandals to match. The look was topped off with dark sunglasses that made her feel like a movie star and a cascade of gold chain necklaces. Knowing the latest fashions was essential, and Marie had learned a thousand tricks to put a cheap outfit together and make it look like new.

She knew which bargain stores carried the best brands on sale and borrowed clothes and jewelry from all her girls. Of course, she picked good customers and knew how to make them feel special enough to treat her to a gift of good jewelry and a trip to the hair salon.

This was her motto: "Look like money and you'll attract money." So far, it had been a true guide, and she stuck to it. Her reputation around the neighborhood was known. Word on the corner was that she was not an ordinary working girl. She was high class.

She and her sisters were raised to keep up that image, "Keep yourselves up, always look nice, and smell clean." That was a law for her and her sisters. Nancy did not play when it came to a clean house and a clean body. Harmony would later be taught the same lessons.

As she walked to the corner to meet Harold, Marie thought on her plans for the week ahead. She knew that her Saturday would be very busy with work. Saturdays had been that way for a while. This was because Friday was payday for most of her tricks.

Friday was a family day, a day for her tricks to pretend to be the perfect husband. By Saturday, they were ready to blow off steam. Saturday was the day to spend the week's hard-earned cash before Sunday came and they had to get ready to start the week all over again.

She wished she could spend all Saturday with Harold instead of working, but that was not going to happen. Marie enjoyed spending time with her new man, but knew that she couldn't keep hanging with him and not get anything up out of it.

She had to devise a scheme to make certain she would be dropped off as soon as brunch was over.

Now that I think about it, I didn't make any money yesterday, she thought. *I can't let that happen again.*

She only had one day that she took off—Sunday. She had vowed to never sell pussy on Sunday. That day belongs to the Lord. Selling pussy on a Sunday would be the biggest sin.

Though some church folk might look on her family as sinners, Marie was raised by a spiritual woman. Her mother, Nancy, raised her own to have faith and pray. Marie was introduced to God at a young age, and though she was prostituting, she believed the Lord knew her heart.

Nancy had raised her daughters to hold their head up high and have the strength to take care of themselves, no matter what. "You don't need no man to take care of you," she told them. "Treat them right and take what you deserve."

I wouldn't have to live this way if he would have blessed me to be like some of those people who grew up with a silver spoon in their mouths, Marie thought to herself.

Make no argument about it, she had to work, and that she would continue to do until something better came along.

By the time she reached the corner, Harold was standing on the passenger side of the car.

He gave her a wide smile and a kiss on the hand.

"Man, oh man, I have got to be the luckiest guy in the world."

"You think so?" she asked. She smoothed down her hair and looked bashful.

"I know so, I know so." Harold gave her a long look up and down before reaching over to open the car door for her.

Such a gentleman, she thought, slipping back in to her treasured place inside that beautiful Cadillac.

For the twenty-minute-ride, they decided to turn the music off and get to know one another better. He told her about the one-year sentence for assault of which he had falsely been accused.

She felt so bad for him because some girl had lied on him when he decided to leave her.

She told him about her life with Nancy and her two kids. He told her that if she and the kids needed anything—anything at all— to let him know and he'd take care of it. Being the hustler that she was, she decided to put it on thick.

She told him how she had to take care of her younger sisters like they were her very own. She didn't leave out the part about them needing summer clothes either.

"I know how that is," said Harold. "The whole time I was coming up, I never had the right clothes for anything. I promised myself that one day, I would wear the finest suits from all the best stores."

He turned to look at her with that glowing smile.

"I usually get what I want."

He waited a moment and said a few last words before turning the radio back on.

"Gorgeous, don't worry about your family. After we leave from eating, I am taking you to Elder-Beerman's to get the kids summer shit."

With the music playing quietly again, Marie daydreamed and watched Dayton pass by from the comfortable interior of the car.

Damn you are good, she thought. *One less thing that I have to worry about and one less day I have to sell ass.*

This was not something that she enjoyed doing, the lying and the selling of her body. She hated both and now was hoping that Harold would supply her with a way out of that madness. Perhaps she could work for him at his store. She would be a great saleswoman. She loved fashion. She could count money well. She also knew how to talk somebody into spending their money.

Brunch was great, but that five-hundred-dollar shopping spree was better. She had never seen a credit card in her life before he pulled one out.

"How would you like to pay, cash or credit?" asked the saleswoman.

"Credit," he replied.

Marie couldn't believe her ears. She had never known anyone who could go to the store and pay with a credit card. She felt like a superstar, and Harold was her sun. It seemed like he had special powers—only he could ensure that a black man with a credit card could walk out of the store without being in handcuffs.

Marie was able to get her two kids and her sisters Stacy, Tracy, and Shell some clothes for the summer. She always looked out for Shell because at seventeen, she was still a good girl, and Marie appreciated her help with Lil' Man and Starla. She wanted to make sure Shell never had to make the choices that her sisters had to make.

Marie thanked Harold for being so good. She also thanked herself for this triumph.

I'm going to have to keep this one around, thought Marie.

After he loaded the bags into the car, Harold closed the trunk and turned to Marie. He smiled and brushed his strong hand down her arm. Turning ever so slightly, he pinned her against the car with a teasing gesture, his body sandwiching hers against the sun-warmed metal of his Cadillac. She could feel how thick and heavy he was as he pressed up against her.

"Oooh, I got you," he grinned and gave her two quick kisses, leaving her wanting more.

Marie giggled and struggled but just enough to press against him so she could feel every inch.

"Oh, no you don't," she laughed.

Enjoying his teasing, she let her curves brush against his hard chest as she pretended to break free.

Harold tightened his grip and leaned over so their cheeks were touching. Marie's breath sped up as his lips gently brushed her earlobe.

"Do I make you happy, Gorgeous?" he spoke low and quiet.

"Yes," murmured Marie.

She stayed still, enjoying the feel of his strong hips holding her against the car.

Harold kissed her quickly on the cheek and let go, stepping back just enough so that Marie was still caged in his arms.

"Good," he smiled. "I'm glad. You keep making me happy, and I will keep making you happy. What do you think, Gorgeous?"

Marie reached up and grabbed Harold's wrists.

"Sounds good to me," she grinned, holding on tight, pulling him close to her body again, and fluttering her famous eyelashes at him. "I think I'm going to make you very happy."

She would make sure of that.

5

Harold gave her a kiss and dropped her off a block away from her house. As she walked toward home, she was a little disappointed at how they had to hide their relationship, but she knew Nancy wouldn't allow her to be messing around with this man, especially with her being a minor under the law. She also knew Harold wasn't ready to be coming in the house either.

She struggled to get the shopping bags through the door and yelled for somebody to come and help her. Shell came running out, along with Stacy and Tracy.

"Marie, how did you get all this stuff from Beerman's?" Shell was always nosy.

"Don't worry about it." Marie waved her hand and picked up the bags to bring them into the house. "Please stop staring and help me carry all these."

Everybody in the house wanted to know how she had got all those outfits. Marie would always come home with shopping bags but nothing like this.

Nancy came to see what all the fuss was about. When she saw the bags of new summer clothes for each of the girls and the kids, she started crying. She was hurt that her daughters had to help her raise her younger three. But she was also happy that she was surrounded by so much love. Living in a small two-bedroom house with nine people wasn't bad at all, as long as love could reside there too.

Marie grabbed Lil' Man and Starla and dressed them up in their new outfits. Starla had on a pink summer dress with matching hairclips that were little bows, and Lil' Man had a fresh white, short-sleeved button-up shirt and a pair of tan leather boots. They looked like they could have come out of the JCPenney catalogue. All the girls marveled at how cute the kids were and how nice their own outfits were.

After enjoying the last few days with her new man, Marie was tempted to spend some time relaxing with her kids. But it was time to get real and get to work.

No sooner than that thought came to mind, she got a beep. While walking to the phone booth, she hoped that more calls would come through so she wouldn't have to keep walking back and forth.

She picked up the pay phone and dialed.

"Hello, did somebody call a pager?" she asked in her professional voice.

An older man's raspy voice came over the line.

"Yeah, sexy, it's me, Elroy. When can I see you? I need you right now. Your daddy needs you right…now."

Part of Marie's game was to stall her clients. She didn't want them to think she was too desperate for their money. Acting like a lady in demand was part of her game.

"How about in half an hour?"

"Why so long, baby? Can't you just get around here and let me make you happy?"

Elroy was a pain in her ass, but he was one of her most regular clients. She hadn't been working regularly for a few days and knew it was time to get down to business.

"I'm on my way," she said.

Marie waited a second to see whether or not she received another call. When nothing came through, she started on her mission to Elroy's. Marie hated this man. She absolutely hated him.

It was hard for her to understand how an old man like Elroy could have ever gotten his beautiful wife, Kay. She really couldn't understand why he had the nerve to cheat. In her book, if anybody should have been cheating, it should have been Kay. His wife was about ten years his junior and was just simply beautiful and nice.

She would come over and give Shell all her old clothes, which weren't old looking at all. She would also do all their hair out of her basement. That's how Marie met Elroy.

A year ago, Kay had asked Marie would she mind keeping an eye on the baby while she ran to get their other children from school. Marie told her she wouldn't mind one bit. Next thing you know, there came Elroy.

"Kay! Kay?" Elroy called from the top of the basement stairs.

"She's not here," replied Marie.

"Who is that?"

"It's Marie, her customer from around the corner."

She heard the stairs creak as he came down into the basement. He walked up until he was in her face. He stared too hard at her, and she didn't like the way he was looking.

"Oh, you're one of Nancy's babies?"

This man was a pastor, and she had to be polite.

"Yes, I'm Nancy's daughter."

"Nancy knows she got some sexy daughters," he said. "What's that one's name that come by here and gets the clothes?" he asked.

"My sister Shell," Marie replied.

"Yeah that's the one. She sure is a cute young thang. Very cute indeed."

Marie did not like the way this man was talking at all.

"If I wasn't afraid of the law, I would put this thing all in her."

"What?" She could not believe her ears.

Pastor Elroy made her feel like that time she reached in the cupboard and accidentally touched a cockroach. *Ugh.* Her skin felt hot just remembering it. She had crushed that thing with a newspaper and threw it on the gas flame to burn.

"I said, if I was her age, I would have her. But since I am a married man and twice her age, she is off limits."

Marie knew that wasn't what he had said at all. She couldn't wait to get home to tell Shell she could no longer come there by herself.

"Sexy, I got a question for you?"

What now? Marie was irritated, but she had to reply. Nancy's training had taught her manners that she had to obey.

"What?"

"Have you ever been penetrated? Do you know what the word *penetrated* mean?"

This man was dirt! She wanted him out of her face. She tried to give him the hint and answered with a tone of disgust.

"No I don't."

"It's when two grown people make one another very happy."

Marie knew what he meant but chose not to respond.

"I would pay a sexy young lady twenty-five dollars to let me make her happy."

"How?" Marie couldn't help wondering.

She was all for making money and was always on the lookout. Money was her road to success, and she was hungry to take that first step.

"Well, if you would allow me to, um, taste what you got in your pants and not tell anybody, I'll give you the money."

By this time, Marie wasn't even surprised at how low that snake was. In fact, she was even a little bit happy at how the tables had turned. To her, it sounded like all she had to do was take her pants off; she didn't even have to mess around with him really, and she would make some money off of this fool.

It was early on in her game, and Marie was just learning her number one rule—"Men are dogs. So play them like they should be played."

She decided to take his money, but she was worried about Kay.

"Your wife will be back any minute."

Looking down at his watch, he said, "No, we still have thirty minutes to do what we got to do."

Marie wanted to say no. She felt disgusted by this man. But twenty-five dollars was a lot of money, more than she had ever earned in her life. She told herself that would be her only time, and she wouldn't have to tell anyone. Against what she felt was her better judgment, she undressed from the waist down and allowed him to try to make her happy.

Between breaths of air which were few and far between, Elroy chewed, sucked, and gnawed at her, over and over. He asked her if he could stick his face in there so he could see the glory of God. She moaned from pain, which he took as yes.

She stared at the ceiling and waited it out, until finally he stopped. She had never felt so grateful to God in all her life. She stood up, drenched from spit. Between her legs felt like it was on fire.

Elroy pulled up his pants and gave her the twenty-five dollars from his pocket. She received her payment and her compliment for "God having created the best organs he had ever seen or tasted."

Marie wiped herself off with some tissues and put her clothes back on, stuffing the hard-earned money in her pocket. She was ready to forget about her hair and leave.

He tried to enter me with nothing but his face, she thought. *How could I be this sore?*

But no sooner than she pulled herself together, she heard the sounds of children coming to the front door. Elroy rushed upstairs to play it off like that's where he had been the entire time. The inside of Marie's pants knew different.

After Kay finished with her hair, Marie decided that she would pay Kay with the money Elroy had given her. She felt that all the pain she had just endured was well worth the ten-dollar tip. She couldn't imagine Kay having to endure that on a regular basis. She deserved that money, plus a well-needed trip to the doctor.

Marie had sworn to herself that that would be the only time. But that one time turned into many more. Each time, she swore it would be the last.

Marie dreaded going to see Elroy. She dreaded it more now than before. She used to feel so bad for Kay. She didn't like going behind Kay's back. It was bad enough she was married to this fake-ass pastor. But Marie could not listen to only her feelings. She needed the money. The only thing that made her happy was when, two years later, Kay left him.

Elroy felt like Marie should pick up where Kay left off.

When her visits to Elroy started, he had to wait until she came and got her hair done. She always paid Kay with the money he gave her. She hoped that Kay wasn't giving him her money. Later she found out her prayers had been answered.

When Marie heard through word on the street that Kay had left Elroy and took the kids and their savings, she gave a little prayer of thanks.

Times had changed. Elroy could no longer buy tight wetness at a cheap rate. Marie didn't believe in any frequent-buyer coupons. It was fifty for oral and a hundred for sex. Elroy didn't mind paying the hundred to feel the "glory of the Lord."

Marie didn't like sleeping with a pastor, not at all. She would pray that God would remove this man out of her life and the lives of many others. She knew this man was nothing but the devil—a devil that knew the Bible from beginning to end.

If the money wasn't good, she wouldn't have given him her pager number. Hesitantly, Marie had given him the number when he'd heard it go off at his house one day. Usually she kept it on silent when she was working as to not disturb her customers. That day, she had been very busy and wanted to get Elroy out of the way. Now Elroy could page her, and she had to go over there, if she wanted a roof over her head and food on the table.

Making it to the front porch, she could see nosy-ass Mrs. Gladys peeking out the window. She couldn't stand that woman. When Kay had finally left, Mrs. Gladys went around telling people in the neighborhood that she left because "Kay caught him with one of those fast girls of Nancy's, but I'm not going to name names."

That woman needed to mind her own business. She didn't know what was in Marie's heart.

Elroy must have heard her walking up the steps because he greeted her through the screen door.

"Hey, sexy."

"Hello," she answered, hating that she had to talk to this man before getting to business.

"Come on in." He opened the door and motioned for her to come in. "Why did it take you so long to get here?"

Inside the house, he sat down on the plastic-covered couch and opened up his bathrobe.

"I have been trying to keep him up," he smiled at her, spreading open his legs to show her what he was so proud of. "I had to let him rest in my hand while I stroked him with my palms."

She wanted to look away from that shriveled little twig. But he was a paying customer, and she had to be the saleswoman.

"I got here as soon as I could," she assured.

"Good to have you," he replied.

She let him push, pull, and grab on her like a used car. She did her usual routine, moaning "Oh yeah, get it baby" and rocking her hips, as he bit, scratched, and growled. He liked to pretend like he was a lion. She let him pretend whatever, as long as it got him off.

She knew how to work him fast enough that it could be over as quick as she needed. One of her tricks was being blessed with a juicy wetness that made men feel the glory and come in seconds. It was usual for her to make a hundred dollars in less than three minutes. She could tell that he was finished when he started snoring.

She rolled out of bed and went to the bathroom to freshen up. After she was dressed, she picked up Elroy's pants from the floor and grabbed his wallet. She decided it was time to raise her rates and took out $150 today.

Her day was done. All she wanted was to go home, bathe, take care of her kids, and wait on Harold to call.

6

IT WAS THREE IN the morning, and Marie tossed and turned. She got up once in a while to see if she had gotten a page from Harold. No luck. Though she had received calls from her regulars, none were from Harold.

Lying by herself in the dark, she could not stop thinking about him.

I hope he's all right, she thought. *I wonder why he didn't call me? If I don't hear from him later today, I'm going to call him.*

Later that afternoon, Marie sat on the steps next to the pay phone on the corner. She stared at all the cars and people passing by, but really she was just fighting back the urge to call Harold. Again.

There was no use in calling a fifth time to leave yet another message. If he was by the phone, he'd see her calls; and if he heard one message, he heard them all because all basically said the same thing.

"Hey, Harold, this is Marie I was calling to see if you were all right, I haven't heard from you."

"It's me again, handsome. I was calling to see if you are all right. Call me when you can."

Walking back home, all kinds of thoughts ran through her mind. She wondered if he had found a new woman or if she had done something wrong on their night out together. Maybe he was working and just too busy to call.

Later, Marie would learn the real reason. Her man truly knew how to get to a woman's heart.

The man was an excellent businessman. He knew exactly how to work a woman. His plan was to shower them with compliments, attention, and gifts. Then once you got them where you want them, you stop. The women will then think that it was something they did and will try mind, body, and soul to make things right.

Marie decided to talk things over with her sisters. When she told Tracy and Stacy about the brunch, the shopping spree, and the disappearance; they tried to make her feel better.

"I don't know, girl," said Shell. "He could be busy. He does have the shop, the club, who knows what else going on—maybe he is going to call you later. Don't press too much."

"Marie, the man is a fool if he doesn't call you," Tracy said. "I've seen what men do to get you to go out with them. He'll call. I know he will."

"Why don't you go talk to Butter?" Stacy said. "She always knows what's going on."

Marie showed up at her friend's apartment with a fifth of Crown, a two liter of pop, and Butter's favorite brand of salt-and-vinegar potato chips.

She knew that once she explained about her new man, Butter might freak. Marie was nervous, but she needed to know what was for real on what really happened with Butter's stepsister. Maybe she could help explain this sudden disappearance as well.

They greeted each other with a hug, Butter holding on to a scarf on her head to keep it from falling off.

"Hey, girl," she said, "I was just braiding my hair. Come on in and keep me company! Tell me what's good. What you been up to?"

"Oh, you know, this and that, making money, taking care of the family," said Marie as she kept herself busy pouring the drinks and opening the chips.

They sipped their drinks and chatted while Butter finished her hair.

When the fifth was half gone, Marie got enough nerve to ask Butter what she really wanted to know.

"So I don't know if you heard, but I've been seeing this new dude lately," she began.

Butter gave her a sideways look and took a long drink from her cup. She crunched an ice cube between her teeth and swallowed.

"Yeah, girl, I did hear something about that. I wanted to hear it from you though. Everybody has been talking about some young girl that was at The Ball with that motherfucker Hitler."

Marie felt her face get hot. "I came here to get the full story from you, girl. I didn't know who he was until we were at the club and they called him Hitler to his face."

"What do you mean?" Butter asked. "How did you go out with some dude and just end up at The Ball with Hitler?"

"Well," said Marie, "you remember that brotha who owned the store on Gettysburg? He gave me that jumpsuit…"

Butter looked up in surprise.

"Yeah?" she said with a curious look on her face. "How he know Hitler?"

Marie sighed. "Girl, he *is* Hitler."

"What!" Butter shouted, shaking her head. "I can't believe this. His name was Harold, right? Damn. I can't believe that's the motherfucker who took Chevonne. He seemed like an okay dude. Like he smelled good and looked like a businessman with a fat wallet. Damn."

"I always heard about Hitler, but I never seen him in person. That was the guy. Huh. Michael went after him and never came back. I know he's dead because of that motherfucker. What happened, Marie? Are you still seeing him?"

"I don't know," said Marie. "It's been a lot going on. I just realized who he was when we got to The Ball the other night. I asked him to take me home, but then we just started talking, he broke out some of that good stuff…I don't know. He does smell good, girl. And he does have a fat wallet. You know, he owns The Ball. Anyway, we just started talking, and I got to know him some. He opened the car door for me. He calls me Gorgeous."

"Damn. Damn." Butter just kept shaking her head. She reached over and lit a cigarette, blowing the smoke out in a hard stream. She tapped out the ash into an empty can.

Marie took a long sip of her drink.

"I can't believe that he took Chevonne, it just seems so crazy. I mean, wasn't it some other dudes she was hanging with, they told her how she could make some money and brought her to Harold? I mean, Hitler. I know Michael was wanting her to work."

"Yeah, I know she went to him looking for work," said Butter. "But damn, I mean, Michael and Chevonne are gone. I know that dude has something to do with it.

"I know, it's fucked up," said Marie. "I don't know what to think."

She reached for a smoke too and poured herself another drink.

They sat together in the quiet apartment.

"I've been trying to call him for the last few days," Marie finally said. "He hasn't picked up the phone. So I don't know what's going on."

"He's playing you, girl," said Butter. "He's a hustler. We know what these dudes are like."

"Yeah, I know," Marie said. "But he seems so different when you get to know him. I have to see him again. Being with him is like…I feel like I'm living another life. A better life. And it's not just a money thing. He treats me good. He wants to get to know me. He even asked about my kids. He spent over $500 on clothes for us!"

"Well," said Butter, "I don't know. I mean, everything I heard about the dude is bad. But it sounds like he is treating you right. I don't know what to think."

"I just want to get out of this place," said Marie. "Maybe I can get a job at his store or the club. He's the first dude I met who has made money on the street and has legit businesses too. He seems smart. I need to get in with someone like that."

"I feel you." Butter knew what it was like working clients. "I just want you to be careful. Don't get played."

"I won't." Marie put out her smoke and dropped it in the can. "I know what I'm doing."

She stood up to go. Butter gave her a hug as they walked to the door.

"Watch your back, girl," she warned her friend.

"I will," said Marie. "You know this is my game."

After all the talk about Harold, Marie decided she needed to spend some time with her family. She couldn't worry about Harold picking up the phone right now. Maybe he was working and couldn't talk. Like she told Butter, she knew how to play the game and win. Sometimes, you just had to be patient and wait.

The house was clean as usual. Shell was sitting at the kitchen table watching Lil' Man and Starla play on the floor.

"Thanks Shell," Marie smiled at her sister. "I got some time to watch my babies."

Marie made them all mac and cheese for dinner. Lil' Man squirted ketchup all over his, and Starla ended up with more noodles in her hair than in her mouth. Marie looked at her two messy babies and smiled.

"You little monsters," she grinned.

"Rrrrr! I'm a monster, and I'm gonna eat you up!" yelled Lil' Man happily, spooning a giant bite into his mouth.

When dinner was over, she wiped off Starla with a damp rag and sent them into the living room to watch cartoons. She put the leftovers in the fridge for Nancy and her sisters, washed the dishes, and made sure the kitchen table was spotless again. If Nancy found even one noodle on the floor, Marie knew there would be some hell. She took out the bleach spray and gave everything one more swipe.

As she was finishing in the kitchen, she heard the little ones acting up. There was a bang, then high-pitched wailing.

"What's going on in here!" Marie threw down the rag and ran into the other room.

"Starla threw my truck!" screamed Lil' Man. "She hit me!"

Starla was on the floor, kicking and wailing with tears rolling down her face. A Tonka truck was across the room.

Marie scooped up both of them and sat on the couch, with Starla on one side and Lil' Man on the other. She wiped off Starla's tears and handed Lil' Man his truck.

"Shhhh," she calmed them down. "Y'all are family. You got to play nice with each other."

Lil' Man sniffled and wiped his nose with the back of his hand.

"Mommy, tell her that's my truck, a truck for boys and not girls," he pouted.

Marie smiled and got up to get the Tonka truck and Starla's favorite doll. She handed them each a toy and sat them back on the floor.

"Okay, baby, you got your truck. Starla, you can play with all the beautiful dolls that mommy got you. See, what about this one? A beautiful doll for a beautiful Starla." She gave her daughter a kiss on her chubby cheek.

Starla was already patting the head of her doll, pretending to rock it to sleep.

Once the little ones were calmed down, Marie decided to go sit on the porch.

"Shell!" Marie yelled. "I'm going out. Can you put the babies to bed soon?"

It was one of the first warm nights of spring, and people were out. The sun hadn't gone down yet, and the air felt great. Marie opened up a beer and leaned back, watching the scenery go by.

She spotted Candice and Trina up the block walking toward her.

"What's up, girl?" loud Trina yelled.

Marie waved back. Nancy's hand had taught her she better not be screaming up and down the block. That wasn't how a lady acted. She waited until they were closer to reply.

"Nothing, what's up with ya'll?"

Candice, Trina, and Butter were the only girls outside of Marie's house who really knew any of her business. They all grew up in Dayton View, and they all went to the same schools. When it was time to fight, these were the girls that got her and her sister's backs.

Marie trusted them with her life. But even still, not all her business.

Trina and Candice came up to the porch.

"It's been forever, girl!" yelled Trina. "I miss you!"

She gave Marie a dramatic hug and sat down next to her. Her eyes kept scanning the street for people she knew.

"Haaaay!" Trina shouted whenever she saw a friend, waving wildly.

Candice smiled quietly and sat down on the other side of Marie. Trina was the loudmouth, but Candice never talked more than she needed to. To most adults, she appeared sneaky; but to Marie and her friends, she was just quiet Candice. Around the neighborhood, she was known as more of a cosigner. She was never the center of the action, but she was always there to back you up.

"So is it true?" Trina turned to Marie with curiosity. "You were out at The Ball with Hitler?"

Trina was a gossip. It puzzled Marie why so many females trusted her with their business. No sooner than they'd confide in her, she'd confide in everybody else.

Though she told your business, she wasn't a liar at all, which is why Marie chose not to tell her everything. If asked to tell the truth and nothing but the truth so help you God, Marie knew that Trina would sing on all of them.

"I mean, it wasn't no thing," said Marie casually. "I met him when I was shopping on Gettysburg, and he asked if I wanted to go out some time. It's whatever. Nothing serious."

She shrugged and took a sip of her beer.

Candice raised her eyebrows a little bit, and she caught her bottom lip between her teeth. She always did that when she was thinking.

"Mmm, mmm, mmm." Trina shook her head. "I can't believe you were out at The Ball, girl! What was it like? Did you get in that nice ride of his? Did y'all knock boots? That man is *fine*. He came to a party once at my cousin Ray's, and, oh my, he looked like he was packing heat in those expensive-ass pants. If you know what I mean."

Marie had to laugh. Trina had no shame.

"He actually treated me like a real lady, opened the car door for me and everything. We had drinks and danced—that's it."

"I hear he's got some of that good, good stuff," Trina kept talking.

"Oh, I don't know about all that." Marie knew she would leave that part of the night out. No way was Trina going to start trying to use her for a connect.

But it was always good to have a friend like her around to share the latest. The news Trina started talking about next surprised Marie and gave her some possible clues about Harold's recent silence.

"Girl, did you hear about Brandon from Fourth Street?"

"No, what happened to him?"

Trina shook her head. "Girl, you know he was into that robbing and stuff. Turns out, he tried to rob some little hustler who work for Hitler. They said Hitler caught that boy last night and busted him all up! Went after him with a bat, broke both his arms and everything."

"For real?"

"Am I lying, Candice?" asked Trina.

"Nope," said Candice quietly, backing up Trina's story.

"Marie, how long have you known me?" asked Trina. "You know I wouldn't lie to you about anything like that."

Marie knew Trina wasn't lying. That's what hurt her most. She just wished he had thought of her enough to call her back. She wasn't just some other girl to get played with. She deserved more.

His violent side didn't really bother her. She knew the rules as much as he did. To get off their street, sometimes you had to do things you weren't proud of. Hitler had power, and he made sure that others knew his rule. He had to protect that. Marie wanted to be a part of that empire—to rule it with him as she knew she could.

She remembered the crowd parting before them as they walked through The Ball and how good it felt with him on the dance floor, wrapped up in his arms, like they were in their own private bubble.

Trina was still talking with Candice, and Marie let her mind wander. Trina was right about one thing—Harold was definitely packing some heat.

His power was so intense. That moment in the parking lot, she had felt every inch of him, demanding her full attention. He knew just how far to go to tease her, and that made her even hungrier for him. She had wanted to jump up on the hood of the car and wrap her legs around him right there. Even with clothes on, she could feel he was thick and heavy and knew just how to use it.

She shifted in her chair. She couldn't wait to find out what he could do to her once they were truly alone.

Harold had said he always got what he wanted. Well, so did she. If he was trying to play a cat-and-mouse game, she would play. She knew that Harold would soon call, and when he did, she wouldn't answer. She said to herself, "Two can play this game."

7

TUESDAY MORNING WAS THE day that she got the chance to test her skills.

After finishing up with one of her regulars, she felt the vibration of her pager go off. To give her client his much-needed attention, she ignored it.

Once she arrived home, she answered the call. As she stared at the number, she knew that it looked familiar, but she also knew that it wasn't any of her clients. After a minute, she realized the number belonged to Harold.

Finally! Marie thought. This was the call that she had been waiting on.

She wanted so badly to hear his voice and for him to explain his disappearance for so many days. But she wouldn't let him think that she was sitting around trying to find out.

Harold had dialed Marie's pager three times and put 911 at the end to let her know that it was imperative that she got back with him ASAP.

She let hours go by and still did not return his calls.

It was getting late. The kids were in bed, and Nancy was in a deep sleep. Marie and her sisters went to sit on the bottom steps of the abandoned house next door, to smoke a much-needed joint and pour some drinks.

Tracy had them cracking up! Everyone in the neighborhood said that girl should be a comedian.

"Y'all remember Ms. Ann!" Tracy laughed the smoke right out her nose as she passed the joint to Shell.

"Oh no." Stacy shook her head, laughing so much she was barely able to keep herself together. "That woman can drink more than any man I know! Too bad she can't be drinking whiskey on Nancy's couch no more!"

They all fell out at that one. Their neighbor Ms. Ann was a sweet woman and one of Nancy's best friends. But when they were all drinking, they couldn't help tell the story; it just made them all laugh too much.

"Nancy, please help me, I peed my pants!" Tracy shouted her imitation of Ms. Ann hollering at the top of her lungs.

"Not on my couch, you didn't!" Stacy blurted out, jumping in to play as clean-freak Nancy's part.

The girls laughed so hard, they had tears rolling down their cheeks.

"You are killing me, girl!" laughed Stacy, wiping her eyes. "That look on Nancy's face was too much!"

Shell passed to Marie and joked, "If y'all don't quit playing, I'm about to pee myself too. I'm laughing too much!"

And that set them all off again.

Marie exhaled a thick cloud of smoke, enjoying the rare time with her sisters.

Suddenly, a canary-yellow Fleetwood rolled up and stopped. Marie knew who it would be, even before the driver-side window rolled down. Her stomach fluttered up into knots.

Harold hung his arm out the window and called over to her, "Hey, baby."

He was playing it cool, but his fingers were drumming the car door.

Marie could tell he was nervous. She pulled herself together.

That's right, she thought to herself, taking a minute and then turning to face him. *This queen bee is leaving a little trail of honey. This man is going to be mine.*

"Hello, stranger," she said.

There was no way she was going to get off the steps and walk over to him.

They stared at each other for a minute. Harold was giving her that same look he had when he saw her for the very first time in her red-and-denim jumpsuit, like she was a prize he couldn't wait to claim for his own.

He got out of the car and walked over.

"I was just driving through the neighborhood and happened to see you," he said casually.

Marie knew better. The drive-by visit was a beginner step in her game. But she just smiled. He looked so good. Staring at him, she couldn't help remembering what it felt like to be by his side at The Ball, just the two of them watching over the world.

"It's good to see you," he said, turning to all her sisters and giving them a beaming smile. "My, my, my. So these are the lovely sisters you were telling me about?"

Stacy, Tracy, and Shell couldn't stop staring. Harold was dressed to perfection, as usual, in a grey suit that shone under the streetlights and diamond studs in his ears to match. His hair was fresh and trimmed to perfection. Everything about him was put together with style.

He took Marie's hand and kissed it. Although he only touched her hand, Marie felt his touch over her whole body. Between her thighs suddenly felt very warm, and she let out a slow breath. He turned to look at her sisters approvingly and introduced himself to them, giving them each a kiss on the hand.

"You two must be the twins," he said to Tracy and Stacy. "I know some brothers who would pay good money for that."

He winked, leaning against the railing of the stairs.

Any other player would have gotten an eye roll for that, but Harold's confidence and charm turned his words sweet, making Tracy and Stacy blush.

"For real though," he continued, "if y'all ever want to party, I can hook you up."

Marie couldn't help but notice how all eyes were always on Harold.

In any conversation, he was the center. He gave off an energy, like a boxer in his prime. Any party he was at, everyone else wanted to be there too.

Harold put his hands in his pockets and jangled his keys. Casually he turned to Marie and said, "Baby girl, come take a ride with me."

Marie's heart jumped so hard, she couldn't answer. She took a long sip of her drink to buy time and play it cool. Tracy, Stacy, and Shell were no help. Harold had worked his magic on them. They could only stare at him, look away like they weren't staring, and then look back. Tracy was doing that lip-biting thing she did when she saw a fine brotha pass on the street.

Marie took one more sip to steady her nerves, then took the joint from Shell and dragged on it, making sure Harold saw the full shape of her lips puffing the end. She exhaled a rich cloud, then gave the girls a little smile as she got up off the stairs.

"I'll be back before Nancy wakes up."

They drove around the streets for a while with the radio playing.

After a while, Harold stopped the car next to an empty playground and cut off the lights.

"Hey, Gorgeous, I missed you so much," he confessed.

"Oh, you did? Why? I never gave you anything to miss."

He turned to look at her.

"All this time I went without seeing your face, it was like everything else was faded. I haven't been able to stop thinking about you, how fine you looked coming into my shop, how much you love your family and want to take care of them. I want to drink Crown with you and dance all night again and wake up and have brunch with you. It all seems day to day, without you there to make my life special."

Who is this man? Marie thought. *He chooses his words wisely. I thought that I was bad when it came to talking, but I may have met my match with this one. I may have met my match indeed.*

"How come you didn't return my calls?" he asked.

"What calls?" she said.

"I beeped you several times earlier."

"Oh, I was busy."

She wasn't about to tell him that she was working. With his connections, he probably knew how she made her money. But she swore to herself that was all over now.

"You haven't been easy to get in touch with yourself," she said with just a hint of ice in her voice.

Let him explain that one, Marie thought.

Harold seemed a little surprised like he wasn't used to females who challenged him. But then he smiled.

"Oooh, you got some fire in you. I like that," he said, his voice dropping into a growl. "You're different than these ordinary hoes out here."

"You know that's right," said Marie. "I don't play."

Her voice had attitude to let him know she meant business. But she couldn't stop her eyes from betraying her true feelings. She was touched by what Harold had said, that he thought she was different—special.

Harold smiled and leaned forward to kiss her. She knew she should play harder to get, but she couldn't stop herself. She took his lower lip, sucking it gently, then moved to match his tongue, which he slipped in and out, teasing her, flicking it against her lips, its tip lapping at her, pressing hard then softening again. His skill was driving her wild.

She had never felt anything like it. She grabbed his thigh and squeezed, wanting to reach for his belt right there.

Harold moaned and broke away.

"Damn, Gorgeous," he breathed heavily.

"Mmmm," she smiled, happy that she was able to match his talents.

He adjusted his pants and cleared his throat, then opened up the glove compartment and took out a joint.

"I love kicking it with you," he smiled.

They passed the joint back and forth. Marie sank into the cloud of the dark car, feeling warm pleasure wash over her body. She ran her tongue over her lips, wanting badly for him to reach over and relieve some of the pressure that was mounting between her legs.

Damn, she thought. *What this man does to me.*

The weed was making them both chill, and she felt more free to be open with him.

"I heard you been taking care of some business," she said. "Some noise about that dude Brandon from Fourth Street."

Harold coughed and sat up more in his seat. "That bastard thought he was going to run off with my money."

His voice got loud and pissed.

"He was trying to say he didn't know that it belonged to me. What's wrong with these fools? They always want somebody else's shit. He shouldn't have touched mine. I told him I killed the last fool who tried that shit."

He was smoking hard on the joint. The look in his eyes was wild, and Marie felt like he had forgotten she was even there. She sat back and waited.

"I'm out here for real, you feel me? Frank would never let some raggedy-ass corner boy take his shit, and neither will I. He taught me everything I know, and I'm going to be the king one day, like him."

Marie had heard of Frank through her uncles, Nancy's brothers. They had their own reputation on the street and talked about Frank with much respect. He was a real OG since back in the day and drove a new Cadillac every six months. After they talked about Frank's newest ride, her uncles usually started discussing the latest woman who was riding inside that fine car.

Harold was still up in his head, ranting and talking about Frank.

"Frank taught me everything I know. He showed me everything—how to collect that money, how to check the traps, always have the best. Best club, best clothes, best cars, best women, best weed, best coke."

Marie sat and waited for him to chill. Whenever a brotha was riled up, it was always best to not make a move, and he would usually calm down. As usual, she was right. After a while, they put out the joint, and Harold let out a deep breath.

He cleared his throat and then reached over to wrap Marie's hand in his. "I'm sorry about that, Gorgeous. I get a lot of pressure on me sometimes. But I know you know what I'm saying. You might be young, but I can tell you are a woman who is on her game. That's what I like about you."

Marie smiled and squeezed his hand. "That's what I like about you too."

He turned to face her. "Is there any way that we could spend twenty-four hours together, starting now?"

8

MARIE RUSHED AROUND THE house packing bags. Harold would be there in an hour.

The time to leave had come quickly. She couldn't believe he had asked her to bring her kids! That was a first. No man had ever included her kids before.

He had wanted her to wake up her kids and bring them over as soon as she agreed to spend the day with him. But she convinced him to wait until morning at least. The kids were asleep; and she needed to take some time to get herself shaved, showered, plucked, primped, lotioned, and perfect. Nancy had taught her the ways of being a true lady who respected her body. Marie was glad for her mother's lessons. She walked out of that bathroom feeling like a queen.

Thank goodness the kids had all those new outfits because she needed enough time to get all her clothes together. She had to have some regular loungewear, but then she needed lingerie, just in case. Marie sorted and re-sorted through her drawers to put together several multipurpose outfits that could go from day to night. She was excited. She couldn't wait to find out what these next twenty-four hours with her new man and her babies would be like.

While she was packing, Shell came into the room, wanting to know what was going on.

"Why are you packing their clothes?" asked Shell.

"Because we are leaving for tonight."

"To go where?"

"Why are you so nosy?" Marie hated having to explain her business to everyone all the time. "I'm grown, and my kids are going with their momma. Is that okay with you?"

"All I am saying is, somebody needs to know where you and the kids are, just in case something happens," replied Shell.

Marie stopped packing for a moment to give her little sister a reassuring smile.

"I'm sorry, Shell. You're right. Harold wants to spend time with me and the kids. Will you cover for me?"

"Wow, he wants the kids to come over too, huh?" said Shell, raising her eyebrows. "That's exciting! What should I tell Momma though? She's gonna kill Harold if he just shows up like he did the other night."

"I know," said Marie. "I told him never show up unannounced like that again. I about freaked when I saw him! You can tell the twins where I am, but tell Momma I'm spending the night at Butter's."

"Will do," Shell replied with a wink. "Just make sure you give me his contact information before you go."

Harold picked up Marie and the kids around the block like she had suggested. She loved seeing how he took charge and buckled the children in. As they drove across town, he handed them the toys he bought them to keep them quiet.

Starla was thrilled with her stuffed pink teddy, and Lil' Man raced his new car around the back seat, making motor noises with his mouth. Marie could tell that they were warming up to him because they asked him one question after another.

"Do you watch Heckle and Jeckel?"

"Do you watch Mighty Mouse?" asked the other.

"Starla, Lil' Man, that's enough," Marie hushed them. "Uncle Harold needs to pay attention to the road."

But she was smiling, and so were they.

By the time they made it to Huber Heights, the children were fast asleep. They carried them into the house together, with one in her arms, and one in his.

I wish that I wouldn't have had children by those two, Marie thought. *They never spent even this much time with me and both my kids.*

Carl, Lil' Man's dad, wouldn't buy his son a toy, let alone spend time with him. Marie didn't see that coming when she made the mistake of naming her firstborn boy after his dad. When she realized her mistake of honoring him with a junior, she and her family bestowed on her son the nickname that she felt best described the boy she had.

Steve was different. He loved his daughter, Starla, very much. But now that he was married, his wife wanted him to just focus on "their family." The woman was so threatened by his and Marie's relationship, even though it had strictly been about Starla.

Anytime he would come and spend time with her, she would come knocking on Marie's door, if he was a minute longer than he said he would be. Finally, Nancy informed Steve's wife that it was indeed her door and that if she ever came back around there knocking on it, she wouldn't leave to tell it.

To see how Harold handled her two babies and their questions made her beam.

After laying the kids down, she now had the opportunity to marvel at what she saw. The house they were in was beautiful! It had two levels, with two living rooms and two bathrooms. One of the living rooms was home to a black leather couch where six red pillows were lounging. The whole room was decked out in black and red. A red dragon and black samurai swords decorated one wall, and everything looked brand-new.

The other living room was clearly Harold's showcase room. It looked like something out of Hollywood. She could tell it was off limits, except for the most special of occasions.

Everything in the room was all white and brass. The sofa in this room was white leather, with a matching love seat. Glass and brass tables accompanied a glass fish tank full of sparkling white fish, and a snow leopard with yellow eyes looked out from the gold-framed painting on the wall. What really caught her attention was the white mink rug that she knew he didn't get from anywhere in Dayton.

She continued wandering on her tour while Harold changed his clothes in the other room.

The bathroom downstairs matched with the black-and-red room. The kitchen was a nice size, but it was a mess. She knew that she would be cleaning it up before tonight was over. There was no way she was going to sleep with a dirty kitchen on her mind.

There was only one thing that interrupted her happiness. There was a pair of black leather high-heel shoes in the downstairs hallway. The decor also was a dead giveaway of a woman's touch. But she could not dwell on that right now. The evening had started off too well for her to be worried about a pair of shoes.

"Gorgeous, may I offer you something to drink?"

Harold walked into the room wearing white linen pants with a white linen shirt, smelling of fresh cologne. The top buttons of his shirt were open, showing off several heavy gold chains and his well-polished tan skin.

"I would like a shot of Crown," she replied.

Marie had liked the smooth taste since their first night drinking together and had promised herself to not drink unless she was drinking the best.

Much of the evening was spent talking about her children and his. They shared stories about their struggles coming up and plans for the future. The Crown went down smooth and easy.

Harold continued to shower her with compliments, and she felt her heart race every time he stared at her with those prize-fighter eyes. It was all she could do not to lean forward and trace the line of those perfectly cut pecks with her tongue.

She loved that he was giving her the power to make the first move. To heighten the pleasure and make him wait, she excused herself to wash his dishes.

"Gorgeous, you're kidding me!" Harold protested with surprise, but Marie also saw a look of delight in his eyes.

This was exactly the level of skill that she was famous for. Men always expected one kind of foreplay. But she knew there was more than one way to give a man pleasure. She liked to mix that pleasure, to give it to a man in more ways than one.

She had learned a thousand different ways to give a man the pleasure he craved. Each trick would give her the result she wanted for herself. With her clients, she knew how to make it fast and keep them coming back for more. With Harold, she wanted the pleasure to go on and on all evening. She wanted him to feel taken care of in his home, in his body, in his mind, and in his heart.

As she stood up to take care of business in the kitchen, she stepped close to the sofa so that her thighs were on either side of his.

She leaned forward, whispering, "I'll be right back."

A thrill ran through her as she noticed Harold's eyes become mesmerized, staring at the luscious gifts presented to him in her silk low-cut top.

She gave him a quick, powerful kiss, catching his lips in hers and enjoying the shiver that ran through her as her hardened nipples brushed against the silk top.

This is going to be fun, she thought.

Harold ran his hands up her thighs and squeezed.

"Ooh, this meat," he growled. "Stay right here. Where you going?"

She smiled and let him hold on for just another second, then pranced away.

She could feel him watching the thick sway of her ass as she padded out of the room.

By the time she came back, Harold had turned the TV off and turned on The Whispers.

Candles supplied all the light they needed. She noticed that the mink rug was no longer held hostage by the coffee table. The fan in the corner made certain she could tell that.

Harold sat on the love seat in nothing but a tight white pair of shorts. He leaned back with the confidence of a man who has nothing to hide. His body was cut to perfection, not too hard but not too soft. His jet-black fro stood neatly at attention. He watched her coming and smiled.

Look at this man's eyes, his nose, his teeth, his lips, Marie thought, staring at him. *He is perfect in every way.*

She sat next to him, and they kissed. She could feel him shiver as she slipped her tongue into his mouth as if sipping a drop of nectar.

"You said last night that you missed me. Tonight is the night that I give to you what would be deeply missed," she said.

She straddled herself on top on him, then slowly used the tip of her tongue to trace each of his eyebrows and kissed the top of his nose. Ever so carefully, she slid her tongue along his lips, gliding it back and forth gently. She needed to taste his flavor.

Harold began to moan and shake under her, rewarding her for her attention.

"Gorgeous," he whispered, "I can't take it anymore."

He wrapped his arms around her as tight as he could, braced himself, and stood up. Still with their tongues entwined, he laid her down on the white mink rug. Now he was in control, and soon she'd see and feel what she'd miss.

Harold started from her head and ended at her toes. He got rid of anything that was in his way. Her shirt was a distraction—it had to go. That bra, though it was sexy, was forbidden. Anything that stood in his way had to go.

The foreplay was unbelievable. She had never taken the time to explore another body this way. Marie finally knew what making love felt like. She finally knew how it felt for a man to really make her happy.

He took her hands and guided them along his body, showing her exactly how he liked to be stroked. She learned his rhythm and watched with pleasure as his eyes closed and he leaned his head back, giving himself over to her. When he began to shake again, he grabbed her wrists to stop her.

"Wait," he commanded. "Now it's my turn."

The beautiful mink rug caressed her skin as she leaned back and let Harold take over.

He gave her a powerful kiss and whispered, "Gorgeous, I want to do for you what I don't do for any other woman."

As he ran his tongue down her body, she shivered with anticipation and had to fling her arm across her mouth and bite down to keep from shouting as his tongue stroked her over and over in gentle circles.

Harold showed her rhythms she had never known before, cooling her down with soft breaths, then surprising her with a deep plunge of his strong tongue that gave her such a shock of pleasure, her legs straightened into the air and she cried out. Over and over, he brought her to the edge, until finally Marie reached for his biceps and pulled him to her.

He entered her body gently, letting her treasure every slow stroke. The more she said "Harold," the further he went. He wanted to explore every wall he could. He tapped on her, and if she moaned, he'd tap harder. He needed to hear her call his name.

Marie couldn't take any more. Tears of joy streamed down her face. She was on the verge of a big release. She felt overwhelmed with pleasure, her body started to shake. She was feeling embarrassed because her legs were uncontrollably shaking.

"That's all right, Gorgeous, let yourself go," Harold whispered.

She did just that.

As her body shook, a stream of water came rushing out from between her legs. The more it came, the more he stroked and moaned.

She felt a sudden panic. *Did I just pee? What would I do if I had peed on his rug?*

"I… I'm sorry," she said, her face hot from embarrassment. "It was an accident…"

Surprise washed over her as she noticed Harold grinning.

He looked at her and said, "Baby, that wasn't an accident, I wanted that to happen."

Happy and satisfied, they lay in one another's arms.

"I like having you in my life, Gorgeous," whispered Harold.

"I like being here," said Marie, giving him a kiss. "I like having you in my life too."

The next morning, Marie woke up in a king-size waterbed. She could hear the children playing and smell food cooking. In no hurry to get up, she decided to daydream about the night before.

She had enjoyed every minute of it, and she wanted more. She could hear Harold telling the kids that pancakes were ready. Both loved pancakes, so it wasn't a surprise for her to hear them running.

She was greeted with breakfast in bed of pancakes, eggs, bacon, sausage, potatoes, and fruit.

"Good morning, Gorgeous!" Harold sang.

"Good morning!" Marie stretched and yawned contentedly.

"Do you like your coffee with cream or sugar?" he asked, smiling.

"Cream and sugar," she winked. "I like my coffee tan and sweet."

"Coming right up."

After breakfast, Marie took the liberty of cleaning up the house while Harold handled his business. She could overhear him talking on the phone to some girl named Princess.

Harold's voice had turned hard.

"What's going on, P?" he demanded. "You came around here last week with only two hundred. That's a problem."

He was pacing back and forth under the dragon painting in the living room.

"You're my main worker. You should be making three times as much. You're costing me a lot of money, woman. I'm losing business to Frank and his tired-ass hoes. You better stop sniffing up my profits. This is your last time fucking up. You bring me two hundred again, your ass is getting beat," he said darkly.

The twins rushed to see what all the fuss was about and found Nancy giving Marie the third degree. They knew it would happen. Nancy had come home looking for the kids, and Shell told her Marie and the kids were spending the night over Butter's.

Her sisters told her that Nancy went on a rampage. She ran out of the house, shouting, "Over my dead body!" She didn't trust Butter's stepfather since he did time in jail for touching Butter where she shouldn't be touched. Nancy said that she didn't want to have to send him to hell for touching hers, but she would.

She took her pistol and walked over there to find out Marie and her grandkids were not there. Upon investigation, she found out who they were with. Nancy never, ever revealed her sources because she never knew when she might need them again.

Nancy came home questioning the twins as well as Shell. She knew all of them knew exactly where Marie was. She had also known none of them would break, but she'd try her luck anyhow.

To no avail, she had given up and gone to sleep. She would have her time with Marie when she and the kids came home.

Marie was furious. She wanted to know who told her mother. She knew that none of her sisters did, but who would? She kept her business to herself or the few with whom she hung. How her mother always found out what they were into was beyond her.

She knew for a fact that her mother was serious about taking the kids, if she found out they were hanging around Harold again. What would Nancy say to him when he asked her to bring them? Marie knew that leaving him alone was not an option, but now she would have to meet him around the corner.

For now, she sat down with her sisters, and they all told each other everything.

"Girl, she tried to pick us for your info all night," said Tracy. "I was going to page you, but I didn't want to ruin your night. Speaking of which, was—"

She broke off talking and leaned forward, waiting for the juicy details.

"Fantastic, breathtaking, darling!" Marie was putting on her favorite Hollywood accent.

"Fill us in and don't leave a thing out," said Stacy.

Marie told them all about the house, how Harold was so good with the kids, and she left no stone unturned giving them the details about his fine body and how good he was at using it.

Her sisters were thrilled that Marie had found someone to love who treated her like she deserved.

"It's like a fairy tale!" said Tracy.

Marie was never the type who believed in fairytales. She knew better than anyone that there was no such story as a prince coming to rescue his princess in her neighborhood. However, she felt that what she and Harold shared was something wonderful. This man loved her, mind, body, and soul.

IT HAD BEEN FOUR months since they moved in together.

Now that she was with Harold, Marie could no longer do her hustle. For the most part, she didn't mind because he kept her and her kids straight, even though the kids still lived with Nancy. The twins were doing what they could, but the majority of the income had always come from Marie.

Harold was trying to do right by the family, but Nancy would not have any of it.

The only issue was Marie could no longer tolerate her mother's disrespect when it came to her man. He would try to give Nancy money for the bills that were constantly on the edge of being turned off. Instead of taking it, Nancy would tell him she didn't want his dirty money. When it came to how her girls brought home the dough, Nancy could fool herself into not asking any questions. But Harold's cash came from another level, and Nancy didn't want to go there.

Marie would go shopping for both houses and wait until Nancy was asleep or gone before she took the food. She would also give all the money that Harold had given her to her sisters.

She loved her life. She loved the house. She loved the clothes. She loved her new car he bought. She loved her family, and she loved her man.

One day, Harold came home and went to work. That's what he called it when he counted all the money that he made for the week. Marie knew that was the time not to bother him.

She would often use that time to go over to Nancy's. Today she didn't feel up to it. She didn't feel well at all. She wasn't certain what was going on, but she hoped it wasn't the flu. She assured herself that she really just needed to lie down.

Lying in bed, she heard Harold cursing and talking to himself in his study.

He slammed the door and came walking down the hall toward the bedroom. When he came in, Marie could see that his eyes had a glazed, angry look. She knew he had been doing coke again and smoking weed. He had been getting that look more and more lately.

He paced back and forth next to the bed, ranting.

"I can't keep taking all these losses," he said angrily. "Here I am taking care of you, your momma, your kids, and your sisters. Princess decided to go work for Frank, and all my customers went to see his girls because of her. How did she have the nerve to walk out on me? The only reason why I ain't gonna kill that bitch is because of my brother. If she wasn't my niece, I'd kill her with my bare hands."

He stopped and looked at Marie with narrow eyes.

"No woman is going to be in this house unless she can earn her keep."

Marie felt herself turn cold.

"I'm sorry," she said. "I know that things have been hard on you. Tomorrow I am going to go look for a job."

Harold laughed a short, hard laugh.

"What job do you think you will possibly get? You don't have an education or experience! Who do you think is going to hire you, huh? Tell me, who?"

Marie didn't know what to say.

"Well, I'll try my best," she said. She just wanted to get a job and make him happy again.

"Please don't be mad," she said, trying to calm him down. "Please don't be mad…"

"Please don't be mad!" he mocked. He was on a roll and was not going to be stopped. "I have lost thousands because of your family.

Your momma doesn't even like me, and every month I'm paying her bills."

All Marie could do was cry. She knew that everything he said was true. This was all her fault. She wondered how would the man she loved ever find it in his heart to forgive her when all she had done was add another burden on to him.

"I'm sorry," said Marie again. "It's all my fault."

Harold stared at her from the doorway. "I should have known that falling in love would make me weak. My heart has done enough damage. I got to think with my head."

He clenched his jaw and let out a sigh, then came across the room and sat next to her on the bed. He leaned in to kiss her on the neck.

"I'm sorry for making you upset, Gorgeous. I'm just under a lot of stress. All I ever wanted to do was make you happy. I knew providing for you as well as your family would give you happiness. There is nothing in this world I wouldn't do to take care of family, and I feel like we are family. I just hope that you feel the same."

Marie was so happy to have her man back.

"I do feel the same way," she said, reaching out to take his hand. "I love you. I am going to do what it takes to make you happy again. Tomorrow I am going to beg somebody to hire me."

"Baby, those jobs ain't no money. The only way that you can stay afloat is by hustling," Harold assured.

"So what can I do?"

Harold looked away as he said, "As bad as it feels to do this, I think that you should hit the track."

Marie felt her heart stop.

She loved him more than life itself. She couldn't imagine ever giving herself to another man. She had blocked out all the others she had been with and told herself that he was her first.

How could he ask her to do this? Marie thought, but at the same time, she knew she was the breadwinner when it came to her family. *Why should they have to suffer because I chose to love?*

She would do anything to make sure her family was taken care of.

If Harold needed her to do this, then she would do it. She didn't want to lose his love or her family for lack of money.

Tears streaming down her face, she looked her man in his face and said, "I will."

"I'm glad you agree," Harold said, looking relieved, reaching to wipe away her tears. "Don't worry, I won't treat you like the rest of those hoes. You're different. You're my leading lady, and nothing will get in the way of that. You will always be my Gorgeous. I want to spend my life with you."

They got ready for bed, and Harold quickly drifted off into a deep sleep.

Marie tossed and turned. She didn't feel good at all. Her stomach was still hurting, and now her head was aching too. She decided to get out of bed and get herself some Tylenol. She glanced at her sleeping soul mate and left the room.

Waiting for the medicine to take its effect, she decided to sit up for a while. She knew tomorrow would be the day that she would have to give her body to another man, and she just needed some time to prepare herself.

Though she had done this in the past, she never feared any harm. She had dealt with her regulars for years, and most were from her neighborhood. She had never sold her body to a complete stranger. She never had to walk a track. All her customers called her.

She couldn't help but think about Nancy finding out. Though she had her suspicions, she never knew how they really received their money. If Nancy ever heard about her walking a track, she'd kill her. Her sisters would tell her to quit and get it like she used to. Marie couldn't forget about the police.

What if I got picked up? How long would I have to stay in jail? What am I going to do? she wondered. *I have to do this, but I will still be keeping my eyes open for a good job. Maybe I can get two jobs?*

Marie could feel the Tylenol and exhaustion settling in. She decided to go to bed. She knew tomorrow she would have to be strong.

Morning came too soon.

Marie felt worse now than she did the day before. Harold was already up, moving around the kitchen and whistling.

As bad as she felt, the smell of coffee and bacon made her smile. That man could cook. She loved the fact that he knew his way around the kitchen. That was another reason they got along. He loved to cook, and she loved to clean. They made a good pair. He would take care of her, and she would take care of him. They would work this out together.

She promised herself that she would make just enough money to get her family straight. Harold would see that she was a good worker and would do what it takes. For them. Maybe she could work her way up, and do some management for him. She had to do what it took.

Forcing herself up, she got her things ready to take a shower. As she washed, she heard the door open.

"You showering, baby?" Harold asked.

She heard his clothes drop to the floor. The shower curtain opened, and he snuck in behind her, already hard.

This man knew what it took to make her body shiver with pleasure, but that particular morning, everything hurt. When he caressed her breasts, they hurt. When he sucked on her nipples, they hurt.

Sex with him had never been horrible before to Marie. He did all the right things and stroked as easy as he could, but with every move he made, she felt discomfort.

"What's wrong, Gorgeous?" Harold whispered to her in the soapy heat. "Usually I have to beg you to let me quit. You're acting like you don't even want me right now."

She pulled away from him and let the shower pour over her body.

"I'm hurting," she said in a quiet voice.

"Hurting how?" he asked, kissing along her neck and pulling her back toward him.

He ran his hands down her back, putting himself between her legs again. His hands moved her body where he wanted it to go, as he pushed himself back inside of her.

"My whole body is hurting," she told him.

She tried to move away again, but he was getting his. She knew she would have to hold out until he was done.

"Okay just give me one…second."

After they finished, he took the soap and rag and washed her body for her. Marie was relieved. She didn't have the strength to do it herself.

Instead of getting dressed after the shower, Marie lay back down. Harold decided to join her.

"What's wrong, Gorgeous?"

"I don't know, I just don't feel well," Marie replied.

"Well, why you don't just get some rest?" Harold said. "I'll get you some clothes out. I know what they'll want to see you in."

Marie decided not to respond. She focused on her aching body. She had not eaten breakfast nor did she want to. She'd rather lie there and heal.

She lay in bed until the early evening, when Harold came into the room to check on her.

"Marie, it's six o'clock! I've been gone for hours, and you're still in bed? It's almost showtime."

Harold was more hyper than usual. It wasn't hard for Marie to notice that.

"You need some of this goody powder to keep you up?"

"Baby, I don't have a headache anymore," she answered him from the bed.

"This isn't for no headache—this is to keep you up."

"Harold, I'm getting up right now," she promised.

"Gorgeous, I still want you to try some of this. This will help you walk the track tonight. I don't know how long we will be out there. We both are going to have to stay up." He looked around with wild eyes, first out the window and then at the large gold watch on his wrist. He wrestled with something in his pocket.

"Get up, my leading lady. We are going to have to watch one another's backs."

"All right, just let me get dressed first." Marie took off the blanket and got to her feet. She let her comfortable pajamas fall to the floor.

After she showered, she went into the bedroom to get herself together. On the bed, she saw a wig, a red lace thong, platform shoes with high wooden heels, and an outfit—a blue-jean-and-red bell-bottom outfit.

She remembered walking toward him and him calling her Gorgeous. How proud she felt twirling in the middle of the store as if it were her own private fashion runway.

Now she would have to wear that same outfit for another man.

Harold was ready to go. He snorted a little extra and held out the bag for her to do the same.

"Let's go," he said. "Tonight is the night that I present to Dayton my leading lady. Gorgeous, are you ready?"

She made herself a line and then did one extra for good measure. It was time to go.

Harold opened the car door for her, then got in on the other side. He was amped up and gave her a pep talk as they drove.

"You look beautiful tonight, Gorgeous. I have to keep knocking down my boys who want to come by. I know they wouldn't be able to stop themselves around you. I'm afraid of what I would do to them if I caught them looking at you. You are truly a prize that can't be resisted," he talked loudly, drumming the steering wheel.

"Frank thinks this game is his. Since Princess went over to his side, he feels like he owns Fifth Street. We're going to show this neighborhood different. This spot is ours. You and me, Gorgeous."

"Do I look okay?" Marie asked.

"Gorgeous, you are simply that."

The bell-bottom outfit clung to her like a glove. She had picked up a few extra pounds, but they hung on her in the right places. She wasn't athletic, but her build was strong.

"How are you feeling?" Harold asked.

"Better."

The powder had done its trick. Her heart raced a little faster, but she didn't feel that fear that she had earlier. As a matter of fact, she felt much better than she had in years. She felt no pain.

Wonderful, she thought. *Simply wonderful.*

"Now I need to give you the rules of this here game," Harold said, interrupting her thoughts. "Check all your traps, meaning be observant. Never get in the car with more than one passenger. Never take less than the going rate. Tell that trick to put the money on the wood, meaning give you the money before anything go down.

"Never suck or fuck without a condom. It shouldn't take you longer than two minutes to do a blow job. I know it's possible because I've timed you. Last but not least, keep your mouth shut. Never let anybody know who you're working for. Keep in mind that I am watching everything, I and my friend don't miss a beat."

She sat in the car and listened to what he said.

"Who is your friend?" she asked.

He pulled out a pair of binoculars from a bag at her feet, assuring her, "These, right here. I got your back. I love you."

"I love you too," said Marie.

The night was chilling. It was already October, and fall was here to stay a while.

Marie watched the busy street go by as they drove. Fifth Street looked more like Hollywood then a street. All the businesses were lit up with signs. There were bars on every corner. There would be more cars that traveled on this street than on Gettysburg, Marie evaluated.

She decided that she would make the spot right in front of the Swat Club. She observed more money come in and out of that place than any other. She also knew that with her class and beauty, she wouldn't be on her post too long.

Harold parked on a corner in a vacant lot.

"I've got good light here," he advised. "Good luck, baby girl. I got you."

He leaned across her and opened the passenger door to let her out.

Marie walked back and forth. She had seen a few other hoes doing it, and she wanted to look seasoned too.

She walked around the block for about half an hour. Suddenly, she saw two girls get out of a car, and they were kind of loud. They screamed back at a man behind the wheel.

"What, you think you gon' get two for the price of one?" said one.

"I don't think so!" said the other.

They both tugged down their tight dresses and walked back toward the corner.

The car sped off, and the girls started walking like she and the rest had been. They walked up to Marie. One of the girls asked her who she worked for.

"Who do I work for?" Marie said with attitude to let them know she wasn't about to be pushed around. "I work for myself and my family."

She rose up her chin and stared them both in the eye.

The girls returned her stare and then stopped to look around at the streetlight-lit corner.

"Girl, you can't be out here unprotected. You got to work for somebody."

"I got protection," said Marie as she kept walking.

"Who do she think she is?" Marie could hear one of the girls say.

In her mind, she mumbled, *I am his leading lady.*

A blue Lincoln came up the street with the headlights off. Marie figured he was trying to get a better view of the area and the women. As Marie caught his eyes, she knew that he'd be coming for her. She put an extra twist to the way she walked and waited patiently to be chosen. She could hear the other girls calling to be noticed, but she knew that she was his target.

As the Lincoln got closer, she saw the man's tweed suit jacket, his blue eyes, and his pale skin.

Her stomach jumped and she felt her heart flutter nervously. She had never been with a white man before.

"Hey, Mama," he called. "I'm looking for some fun tonight. Do you need a ride?"

"Yes, Daddy, I sure do," she replied.

Daddy—what just made me call him that? Marie wondered.

She had never called her own father that. She shook her head. She didn't have time to argue with herself—it was time to work. She opened the passenger door and got in. The man smiled at her nervously.

"Henry's the name."

"Lady is mine."

"Lady, Henry's been working real hard, and he needs some stimulation."

Marie was trying to figure out if Henry was his name or the name of his penis because he was talking like it was a third person in the car.

"Well, Henry, what you like for Lady to do for you?"

"Henry wants her to put her mouth on him so he can release all the pressure."

"Tell Henry that'll be fifty."

"Fifty? I've never had to pay more than twenty."

"You've never had me."

"Are you that good?"

She let her tongue peek out and ran it softly along her lips, then winked. "Better than good."

He gave her the money and pulled in the alley.

He quickly unbuckled his pants and pulled down his shorts. Marie bit her lips to hold back a giggle. She didn't realize his thing would be so pink!

Henry was breathing quickly and had his head back against the seat with his eyes closed. She leaned in to give him the release from the long day of work that he'd paid her for. It didn't take a second for her achieve his goal. She used her tricks of the trade wisely and used them to her advantage, brushing her fingers lightly against the sensitive tip, then using the condom to tease him as she slipped it on.

He shivered as she swiftly leaned in and rolled it down the rest of the way with her mouth, letting him enjoy the fullness of her lips. He was small, and she took care of him easily.

If more came like him, I'll be out of here in no time, Marie thought.

More customers came. Many of them fussed about the price, but Marie knew what she was worth and she wouldn't waver.

Harold hadn't known that she had already placed a price tag on herself, and she wasn't about to let him devalue her worth. He thought she was working for him, but really she was working for her.

Walking around the block that night, she made a plan. She would give him the twenty that he expected from doing a personal, but she'd keep the thirty for herself. She'd give him the forty for sex and pocket the sixty. She knew that the money she gave him went toward their living expenses. To her, she was still benefiting from the money she basically let him hold.

Though she really did love Harold, she had to stick with the first commandment of her own bible—"Never sell this pussy for no man."

The night went well into the morning. She was exhausted, and so was he.

She was grateful when she finally walked back to the lot and got in the Fleetwood. She handed him a stack of cash. She made no mention of the extra folded up and hidden in her shoe.

"Gorgeous, you did good. You did real good!" he smiled. "I stopped counting the cars once you got to nine. If we keep working together, all my old customers will be back. Frank will have to find him another track to put his hoes on. We make a good team, Gorgeous."

"Daddy, everything I do is for us," she said.

"So I'm Daddy now?" He looked over at her as he drove them home. "I like the sound of that."

She leaned her head back against the seat and closed her eyes. "Daddy, I'm so tired."

"All right, Gorgeous, Daddy's about to take you home."

When they got back to Huber Heights, Harold hurried Marie in the house. He tucked her in the spare bedroom, closed the door, and then walked off to the other bedroom.

Marie woke up sick, her stomach felt nauseated. She ran as fast as she could to the bathroom. She barely made it before what seemed like her insides came up.

After she finished, she ran some bathwater. She needed to soak away the night before. She lay in the tub a long time.

$$\longrightarrow \quad 10 \quad \longleftarrow$$

SHE WOKE UP LATER that afternoon still not feeling well, but she pulled herself together. She decided to get dressed and go hide the money she had made over at Nancy's. She knew her children missed her, and she missed them.

When she arrived, Lil' Man ran and jumped in her arms. Starla followed right behind. Marie burst into tears.

As Lil' Man tried to wipe them away, he said, "Mommy, why are you crying? Aren't you happy to see me?"

At that very moment, Marie hated ever meeting Harold. She blamed herself for falling in love. She should have gotten out when she could. She stayed the whole day enjoying her children and the family.

Nancy made them both a cup of coffee, and they sat down at the table, watching Lil' Man and Starla build a tower out of blocks.

"This is our castle. Starla is the princess, and I am the king," announced Lil' Man, waving his plastic sword.

Nancy looked over at her daughter and smiled. "It's so nice getting to spend time with you, baby. Please promise me you are taking care of yourself."

"I am, Momma," promised Marie. "I've got a new car, a beautiful home…we are making it work. Don't worry. You taught me how to take care of business."

She reached over and placed her hand on top of her mother's and smiled to reassure her.

Nancy sighed. "Whenever you get tired of his shit, you can always come home."

"Thank you, Momma," said Marie.

Nancy still had a worried look. She stared at Marie for a moment and then said, "Are you feeling okay? You look, well…your face has that look. Like you are pregnant."

Marie felt all the blood rush to her cheeks.

"No!" she swore. "Don't worry about it, Momma. I'm fine."

But deep down, she knew she wasn't sure.

It was getting late, and Marie knew she had to end it and head home. She made it a point to tuck her own kids into bed and promised that she'd be back to do it from then on.

When she got back to Huber Heights, Harold was sitting on his black sofa, staring at the clock. Powder was dusted all over the coffee table in front of him, and a blunt was burning in the ashtray. Marie slipped inside quietly to avoid attracting his attention, but she did not get far.

"Where have you been?" he demanded. "It is almost showtime, and you were nowhere to be found."

"Hi, Daddy," she said.

"Where you been?" He watched her from the couch.

"Over at Momma's."

"Next time get here earlier," he ordered.

"That's what I wanted to talk to you about." She looked away from him as she spoke. "I need to start tucking my babies in at night."

"Well, bring them home and quit letting your mother run you."

"She's not running me—she just wants what's best for the kids."

"You mean to tell me that shit getting cut off is the best for your kids?"

"I am saying that she knows that you are a pimp and a hustler, and she don't want my kids involved in it."

"How your momma know my business?" he shouted.

"I don't know, somebody told her!" she yelled back.

Before she knew it, he had rushed at her, picked her up by her throat, and dropped her midair.

He stood over her as she lay on the ground, coughing and trying to catch her breath.

She stared back at Harold with blank eyes as he demanded, "Bitch, don't ever let me hear about somebody knowing my business. From now on, you don't speak unless I give the okay. Get dressed. We got a show to do."

From that day forth, Marie did exactly what she was told. She obeyed his every command, but she knew that it would be short-lived.

He made her get high on powder, even if she didn't want any. Coke became her best friend. With it, she didn't have to focus on not seeing her kids; without it, she felt like committing suicide; on days when Harold pushed her to the limit, homicide. It was best to keep cocaine close.

Harold had told her that five hundred was her target amount every day. In order for her to not slip up, she was pulling double shifts when she didn't have to. She couldn't let on that she was making more money than he thought. She desperately had to.

She had devised a plan that she would save five thousand so she could leave him after he totally disrespected Nancy and her sisters the month before.

It was Thanksgiving Day. Nancy wanted all her family together under one roof.

After several failed attempts of reaching Marie or Harold, she decided to make a surprise visit, with her daughters and Marie's children in tow.

She figured she would make all the thanksgiving trimmings and pack them right along.

"Since Harold won't bring my daughter home for thanksgiving, I'll take thanksgiving to her," she said aloud.

She made sure that Lil' Man and Starla were dressed in the cutest little outfits—he in the baby blue suit he had worn for Easter, she in a red-and-white dress, which came with a huge red-and-white bow to accessorize her afro puff. Nancy herself put on her finest attire, a blue chiffon dress that Marie got her for her birthday some time ago. Tracy, Stacy, and Shell each wore something with the same color blue.

"Momma, do you think we should pack the steel, just in case that asshole act up?" said Tracy jokingly.

"Not at all," Nancy chuckled. "Not at all."

Nancy was positive that this was going to be the beginning of a new start. Surely after Harold witnessed her break her promise of never stepping foot in his door, he and she could extend an olive branch and start over—at least, that was her hope.

She realized that fighting with him caused her to lose her daughter. This also caused Marie's children to lose their mother. Although she still didn't think anything good about Harold's character, she knew her opinions didn't matter at that point—having her family back did.

They each piled up in the grey minivan that Tracy borrowed from one of her regulars. After what seemed a like a journey from Dayton View to the Huber Heights suburbs, they managed to find a parking space in the parking lot adjacent to Harold's condo.

When Lil' Man was where they were, he was so excited.

"Yay! We are going to see mommy!" he shouted.

Starla awakened from her nap, screaming, "Mom...mie! Mommy!"

Nancy couldn't hold back the tears and smile.

"Shhh," she whispered. "Let's not ruin the surprise."

They each grabbed all their two hands could and managed to empty the van in one trip. Before she reached the door, Nancy prayed and asked God to please help her.

Knock, knock.

"Who is it!" said a man with a very loud and disturbing voice.

"It's Nancy."

Harold opened the door with just his green silk pajamas on.

"What are you knocking on my door for?"

"Well, Happy Thanksgiving to you to," Nancy said.

"Mommie! Mommie!" said Starla.

"Tell her to shut up!" Harold protested. "We can't have all that screaming out here."

"Calm down, Starla. You'll see your mommy shortly," said Shell.

"No she won't!" Harold said matter-of-factly.

Not liking how things were going, Nancy had to think fast.

"Harold, I just wanted to come out here and personally apologize," she began. "I was so wrong about you. I never gave you a fair shot..."

"Damn right you didn't!" Harold said. "You never thanked me for all the shit I did for you and your kids either!"

"You are absolutely right."

"I know I'm right, I know I am right!" said a disgruntled Harold. "All you ever did was be an ungrateful bitch!"

Before Nancy could try to charge him, Marie came up behind him.

"Harold, please stop!"

Nancy was in complete disbelief. She hardly recognized her daughter. Marie had lost thirty pounds, tops. She was rail thin, and she looked worn out.

With tears streaming down Nancy's face, she managed to say, "Come home."

"Mom..."

Before Marie could get the rest out, Harold yelled, "She ain't going nowhere!"

He shoved Marie to the ground and slammed the door in their faces.

A usually protective Nancy stood there in agony. She was wise enough to know that it would be worse on her daughter if she pushed the matter.

That was something she definitely did not want. She wanted so badly to kick that door down and beat that no-good idiot up. She was certain that underneath all his toughness, he was a coward.

Instead, she turned around and told her angry daughters and crying grandkids, "Let's go."

Marie was pacing the living room floor. *Here it is, December, and I still haven't been able to see my kids.*

After Nancy showed up on their doorstep, things had been hell. Harold beat her so bad that he broke her nose and her leg.

She had to be rushed to the emergency room. The whole time they were en route, he told her to tell the doctor that she fell. She thought about telling the truth, but she was too afraid of the outcome.

Now that she was all well, she knew that it was time to put her plan into motion. She knew that this time around, she had to move in silence. The last time she threatened to leave, it didn't go well.

"Bitch, if you know what's best for you, you'll sit your ass down and stop playing with me," Harold warned her.

She would do just that. Until the time was right.

She hated him now. She hated everything about the man she once loved. She hated to hear him breathe, hated the way he smiled, and smelled. All were things that she used to adore. Sex with him felt so disgusting. He was so rough and would ask her questions like "Can they do it better than me?"

Every morning, she woke up sick. She didn't know if it was from the cocaine or not. She knew that she had constant draining from her nose, and she wondered if that was from her being sick. When she accidentally hit her breast while she was showering, she knew that wasn't the case at all. The tenderness confirmed it for Marie. She was pregnant. She knew this feeling all too well. Before, she was in denial, but now she was positive.

She stepped out of the shower and wrapped herself in a towel, drying off before she had to get dressed for work.

"Gorgeous?" Harold called from the bedroom.

"Yes?" She hugged the towel tighter around her body.

"Here, I got some fire in."

She walked into the bedroom with her hair still dripping wet.

"You don't need to do two lines of this." He looked up from the piece of mirror in his hand; his eyes looked like black beads. "Just do one or you'll bust your nostrils. This shit is just that pure."

"I can't," she said.

He stopped in the middle of bending his head back down to the mirror in his hand.

"What you mean you can't? I told you that it's that good stuff."

"I'm pregnant," she sighed. She stopped and stood there halfway between the bathroom and Harold.

"Pregnant? How did that happen? I told you to use condoms!"

"Harold, I am pregnant with your baby—with our baby."

"You're going to have to get an abortion," he said firmly. "I can't afford another mouth to feed, and you can't afford to quit working."

Marie felt that cold feeling in her stomach again, a feeling she had felt all too often lately. It was time to put her foot down.

"No." Her voice was so flat and so sure that Harold looked up at her in silence.

They both sat on the bed. Marie was still in her towel. He had the mirror on the bedside table and was looking out the window. Finally, he said something to her.

"Marie, look, we can have the baby, but you're still going to work."

"I can't work," she responded, still sitting on the side of the bed. "Why don't you find somebody else until I have the baby?"

"All right." He nodded and got up, going to the closet. "But until I do, I need you to work."

He picked out a hanger and went over to lay her outfit next to her on the bed.

Her hand came down and touched the hanger. She unwrapped the towel.

"I am not working much longer."

The next morning, Marie took time to call her family doctor. Her appointment was set for the next day. She sat down at the kitchen table and wrote the date and time of the appointment on the back of an envelope.

Sitting there, she thought long and hard about how she would break the news to Nancy. She knew in her heart that Nancy would want to take this baby also. Harold and her momma had their differences, but the baby she was carrying was family.

Harold had met his match when it came to her family. This was war, and they would win. They would keep this baby.

"Ms. James, the doctor is ready to see you." The nurse came into the waiting room, a chubby white girl wearing baby-blue scrubs.

She led Marie into the examination room. Marie sat down on the table covered in crisp white paper.

"Change into the gown on your left."

Marie changed and sat nervously on the cold table until there was a knock and the door opened slowly.

"Hello, Dr. Stevenson!"

Dr. Stevenson came in with his always-reassuring smile.

"How are you Ms. James? Fine, I hope."

He bustled around the room, getting his equipment together. Then he sat down with his clipboard, crossed his legs, and looked at Marie.

"How are my favorite children?" he asked.

"They're great," she replied.

Marie felt bad for lying to Dr. Stevenson. Fact was, she hadn't seen her children in months. She didn't know if they were fine.

She had looked up to Dr. Stevenson since she was a little girl. He had been the one to deliver her and all her sisters. She wouldn't allow any other doctor to see her when she was pregnant. Dr. Stevenson wasn't just her doctor—he was her friend.

After he finished his exam, he wrote something down on his clipboard, put down his pen, and then looked up at her.

"Well, I take it you already know you are pregnant."

"I figured," she sighed.

"I'd say you are about twenty weeks along."

"Four months?" Marie looked at him in surprise.

"Yes!" He smiled and looked at the light curve of her belly. "You are really small compared to your other pregnancies. Is everything okay at home?"

"Yes," Marie decided to lie again.

She plucked at the hem of the light cotton gown when she answered, not able to look him in the eye.

"Okay, I want to see you back here in two weeks. Try to eat as much as you can before then."

"All right, Doc."

"Okay, you." He gave her a pat on the back.

Harold had dozed off in the waiting area. When he saw Marie coming, he stood up and led her by the elbow outside.

"So what did he say, Gorgeous?"

"I am four months along."

"Four months! You're not going to be able to work much longer."

"I can't work at all, and he said that I am underweight."

"How he figure that? You eat."

"Yeah. When I'm not getting high. I have to quit."

"Wait one minute!" Harold hissed dangerously in her ear, gripping her elbow tighter and yanking her close. "Don't come talking no bullshit to me. Bitch, I'll knock your head off. You're going to work until I tell you to stop."

—— ❦ 11 ❦ ——

Harmony

At 4:22 a.m., the baby girl arrived. Her birth had been painful but not very long. Marie felt tired but content to lie there, feeling the tiny heartbeat against her chest.

She and Harold were no longer together. Even still, Marie wanted him to walk through the door. He hadn't.

She kissed her baby's fingers and said, "I guess he's the one who's missing out."

Suddenly, the hospital door opened, and Nancy and all the girls came in. Tracy rushed in first and gave Marie a bouquet of red roses with baby's breath wrapped in pink plastic. She picked up the new baby and squealed. Stacy came in after her and smothered the little face in kisses.

Shell gave Marie a small, white teddy bear and slipped a pink ribbon headband on the baby's tiny, fuzzy head. Butter rushed in and gave Marie a big kiss on the cheek.

"She's so cute," they all marveled.

"What are you going to name her?" Nancy asked as she sat on the edge of Marie's bed, holding the sleeping baby girl.

Marie had thought of many names, but none fit her little girl. She felt like the baby had gone through so much while living inside her. Though she quit using cocaine, she worried that her earlier use could have caused her baby harm. She also thought about how Harold would beat her.

Marie remembered all the times she was pushed, punched, or smacked to the ground on many occasions, all without notice. She knew that the baby could have easily been lost. Instead, God kept her safe. She needed a name that fit. She wanted her to have a name with meaning, for she truly was a blessing to be here.

"Harmony."

Nancy, Tracy, Stacy, Shell, and Butter looked at her.

"Harmony Nicole James," said Marie. "That's her name."

"That's beautiful," said Stacy.

"Harmony. Har…mony," Nancy said, giving Marie an eagle-eyed look. "You're not naming her after that horrible excuse of a man, are you?"

"In a way, I guess I am," said Marie.

Marie wondered to herself why she'd name her daughter after the man who almost caused both their deaths. He had caused her heartache so many times. Moving his new trick Dianne in with them right after she told him she was pregnant had been the final straw.

Harold had told Marie that Dianne was just down on her luck, that she needed a place to stay for a while. Marie knew that it wasn't up for discussion. Especially when it came to Harold's hoes, he took care of business and did what he wanted.

Though everything was done in secret, Marie knew something was going on. Harold would get out their bed in the middle of the night and go to the spare bedroom with Dianne. Marie would pretend to be asleep and would have to hear them making love in the other room.

The worst of it was him sneaking back in to bed like nothing had happened. The smell would literally make her nauseous. This went on for a whole month.

One night, she couldn't take anymore. She called headquarters and told Tracy and Stacy she was coming home. She'd pack all her things and throw them out the upstairs window. The next night, she waited until Harold snuck out of bed. She could hear the sound of bedsprings and a female's low moaning. Marie got out of bed and headed downstairs to the kitchen.

Quietly, she got out a pot, then looked through the cabinets to get what she needed. Her hands shook as she tried to stay quiet and not spoil the little surprise she was cooking up.

In her pot, she boiled a mixture of oatmeal, honey, and syrup. It reminded Marie of when Nancy used to make them breakfast before school. She and her sisters used to hate that oatmeal and would pretend it was Lucky Charms, with those magical, sugary rainbows and clovers.

When the mixture was hot enough, Marie grabbed the pot and carried it upstairs. She could hear Harold panting and grunting from behind the closed door. She grabbed the doorknob and yanked the door open.

Diane's legs were wrapped around Harold's waist, her ankles locked around the cheeks of his bare ass. They were both rocking the bed so hard, they didn't even hear the door open. Anger and hurt filled her as she saw the bed shake with their betrayal.

Marie rushed forward with the pot in her hand and threw the boiling, sticky oatmeal right onto Harold's naked pumping ass.

"You would have thought he had died and went to hell," Marie told her sisters when she ran out into the waiting car. "That's how loud he screamed!"

They laughed, proud of their sister for winning this round. Nancy didn't raise no suckers. They gave one another high fives and drove home.

And even still, sitting in the hospital, staring at the face of baby Harmony, Marie found herself wishing that Harold would forgive her. She wanted him to be the caring father that she knew he could be.

Over the next few months, Harold would come in and out of Marie and her baby's life. If she did what he wanted, then he loved her and their child. If she didn't, it was, "Take your baby and get the fuck out of my face."

Finally, she had enough and left him for good.

She had saved up enough money while she was working with Harold that she could take a little time off. She spent her days going on walks and taking her three kids to the park.

It was a beautiful thing to sit there holding her new baby, watching Lil' Man run up and down the slides, with Starla following him around, copying all his moves.

Sometimes, she worried about her old life and whether her kids would be okay. She was noticing around this time that Harmony would suck on her left wrist a lot. She had taken her to see the doctor because she felt that it wasn't normal.

She was hoping that her doing coke while pregnant with her had nothing to do with it.

Dr. Stevenson told her not to worry, that sometimes children did this for security. He assured her that the baby would grow out of it.

Marie was relieved.

Even still, some days she felt a little bored and missed her old life. She used to feel so glamorous, dressing up in the best outfits and being at the center of all the excitement.

One day, she even put on her best wig, her favorite feather earrings, and a cute black jumpsuit with heels and wore it around the house. But it wasn't the same. She went back to sweatpants and a scarf wrapped around her head.

She got used to her regular routine at the park. One man in particular came there every day at the same time she was there.

He would usually stop whatever he was doing to talk to her. He told her his name was Miller. She told him hers. He'd ask her personal questions like, "Are those your kids? Where is their daddy at?"

Marie didn't mind small talk but felt that he was sort of prying in her business.

She couldn't help but notice that he was a good-looking brother, but Marie didn't want to mess around with any man for a while. Curious, she asked Butter and Trina about him and found out that he had just gotten out of a relationship with his high school sweetheart.

"She gave him a Dear John letter, stating that she was bored with the relationship," said Butter.

"Really? That's so sad," sighed Marie

"Uh huh, and, girl…if you're interested, you need to stop playing hard to get because a lot of females want to grab him for their own. They heard how he always treated her right. He never cheated or laid a hand on her."

Still, Marie was on break and wasn't interested.

One day, while driving Nancy to the store, Marie noticed Miller beside her.

"I can't stand that man," Marie said, looking at him through the window as they drove past.

"Why not?" asked Nancy.

"Momma, every time he sees me with the kids, he bothers me."

"He might like you."

"He has a girlfriend. I don't know how she puts up with him."

"Maybe you'll be surprised."

Nancy was still hoping for all of her daughters to get a good man one day. She didn't want them to wind up like her—struggling to take care of a house full of babies on her own.

Miller blew his horn and motioned for her to pull over.

"I am not pulling over for him." Marie kept her eyes on the road and pretended she didn't notice his lights flashing.

"Pull over." Nancy looked through the window right at Miller. "It might be important."

Marie sighed but decided to pull over. She turned off on the nearest side street and cut the engine. Her mother rolled down her window as Miller got out of his car and approached them. He leaned in with a friendly smile.

"Hello, beautiful ladies," he said. "I just wanted to let you know that your rear tire is low. If you go to the nearest gas station, I will put some air in it."

"Thanks," said Marie.

Nancy looked at her and smiled. She had always taught her daughters to appreciate a man who took care of women.

"No problem," Miller said. "Marie, would you like to go out sometime?"

He saw some hesitation in her body language.

"I am not going to disappoint you," he added.

Marie was moved by his reassurance and said, "Yes. Yes, I will go out with you."

Their date at Ponderosa went off without a hitch. They talked and laughed for hours. On her drive home, she hoped that she'd see him again. After their conversation, she had second thoughts about being so honest with him about her life. Their stories of their upbringing were so different. She had learned that he grew up in a two-parent home—something she couldn't relate to.

His parents were happily married. That was something else that they didn't have in common. Marie never saw her mother in a healthy, loving relationship. She also never knew her real father at all.

Both of Miller's parents were college graduates. His dad was an engineer; his mom a nurse at the very hospital that Marie had her children. Miller followed in his father's footsteps and became an engineer himself. He recently landed a job at General Motors. He had his own apartment, his own car, and had no children to support—he had it all. At least, he had the life that Marie wanted for herself and her children.

After she told him about her mother being an alcoholic and that she and her sisters sold their bodies to pay the bills, she told him about all her failed relationships—how, though it was hard sometimes, she didn't regret having her children. She also told him about her drug use.

Though he reassured her that things would get better, it was hard for her to believe him.

"Thanks for sharing your struggles with me," Miller reassured. "I hate that you had to go through all that. Marie, if you'd allow me to, I'll be there for you. I want you to also know that I am not perfect either."

Marie looked him in his hazel eyes, seeing the sincerity behind his words.

"Thanks," Marie said.

"Will I see you soon?" he asked.

"Sure thing."

He grabbed her car door and motioned for her to get in. Her drive home was an emotional one. She had finally released all the hurt, anger, and fear she'd been carrying inside her for years.

She vowed that she would do all she could to make sure that her children had a different life. She vowed to make certain that they got a proper education. She never wanted them to have to go down the same road she did.

Marie went to apply for welfare and housing. It took a lot of pride for her to do. She never wanted any government handouts. She felt that was in place for people who were lazy. She also felt like the welfare people were too darn nosy.

"How many children do you have?" the lady behind the desk asked.

"I have three."

"Wow, how old are they?"

After that, she wanted to know their ages.

"Where is the daddy?"

"It's three different fathers."

"It's three!" the welfare lady said as she popped her chewing gum.

"Yes, ma'am."

As the woman shook her head, she began using a calculator.

"Well, Marie, you will get four hundred in cash and six hundred in food stamps," the lady said. "Both will come in the mail on the first of every month. Please try to find employment, and don't have any more kids that you can't afford. Your apartment will be ready in sixty days as well."

"Thanks a lot," Marie said as she got up and walked out.

Miller was true to his word. He came to Princeton Park while Marie was there with her children. Lil' Man was pushing Harmony on a swing, while Starla played with some other kids who were there.

"Hey, pretty lady."

His smile was so sexy to her. It showed off his straight white teeth and dimples. Marie couldn't help but wear her excitement on her face. He was looking good. His white silk shorts and matching shirt was neatly pressed. His afro was freshly shaped up as well.

Marie settled on a pink-and-white striped top, with a pair of pink knickers. She wore her hair in a casual bun.

"Hey, I was hoping I caught you here," said Miller. "I have been coming up here at the same time every day, but you hadn't showed…I apologize."

"I have been working over time," Marie said.

"I am trying to get things ready for you and the kids."

Did I just hear him correctly? Marie thought.

"What do you mean?"

"Can we go sit down over there?" he asked.

The wooden bench was a little beat-up. Marie took a napkin out of her purse and wiped it off. She then took the light blanket she had and unfolded it. She preceded to lay it across the bench so nothing would get on his outfit.

Sitting there, he grabbed her hand gently, looking her straight in the eyes.

"Now, back to what I was saying. I know that I have been missing for a month, but it was for a great reason. I have been getting the apartment together for you and the kids."

"Miller…"

"Wait, please let me finish. When you shared things with me about how many people are living in your mother's home, how you are struggling to make ends meet…"

"Miller, I didn't tell you so you could feel sorry for me!"

"I know, I know," he assured. "It just made me care that much more. It caused me to think about what I was missing out on, like not having you and the kids with me."

Marie knew that her mother was telling the truth when she said that it was impossible to know someone well after twenty days of dating. She also knew going to live with Miller was a risky move, especially because she was bringing her children. But something inside her told her that it was for the best.

"Starla, I told you that whatever I say goes," yelled Marie.

"That baby isn't doing a thang wrong," said a drunken Nancy. "You're just picking on her."

"Momma, why would I pick on my baby? She was in the kitchen messing with that hot stove!"

"She's probley hungry. You been sleep all morning!"

In fact, Marie had awakened later than usual, partly because she had pulled an all-nighter with Miller and a couple of his friends from work.

He called her earlier the day before.

"Would you be interested in meeting some of my close friends from the General Motors plant?"

"Of course I would!" Marie said, thrilled.

He picked her up around three that afternoon. She gave Shell fifty dollars for watching the kids. Her plan was to hang out for a little, then come back home in time for dinner. She truly lost track of time.

She had no clue that his friends were party animals. She had been nervously awaiting their arrival. She sat on Miller's couch, rocking her legs back and forth.

"Calm down, little lady. I promise, you have nothing to worry about," said Miller. "They are just like us."

"I'm calm. I think I just need a little bit to calm me down," she said.

"Let's wait on that. I want them to meet you sober."

"What's that supposed to mean?"

"That means I want you to just sit there and be innocent, Marie," Miller said, as he kissed her forehead and touched her cheek.

Knock, knock.

"Open up!" said the husky white guy through the screen door.

"Yeah, open up, my man. Let us in!" said another friend.

Marie knew it was showtime. She had to show them that she could fit in. Although she was fully aware that they were from a different side of the track than she was, she was no stranger to being around white people. She didn't consider sleeping with a white man the same as hanging out. This would be her first time hanging out with them, professional ones who seemed to have it all together. Those kinds always seemed out of reach.

"Ahh, Chuck! Ahh, Boston, come on in!"

Just as soon as they entered the apartment, they immediately locked the screen and closed and locked the freshly painted wood door. Marie couldn't help but notice that the pair looked a little nervous to her as they all locked eyes.

"Hello," she said to break the ice.

"Hey! You must be Marie."

"I am," she said with a smile.

"Well, I am Boston," said the husky guy.

"I am Chuck," the fidgety guy with the receding hairline said.

"Now, since everybody has met, let's get this party started!" said Miller.

Marie couldn't believe it. Just like that, his friends were pulling out coke and weed.

Chuck actually rolled his weed and coke up together. That was Marie's first time seeing someone do it that way. She nudged Miller and told him that it stunk so bad.

He told her that he agreed, but he just told her to try to grin and bear it. He told her that Chuck was the president of the company's son.

They all consumed more drugs then Marie ever had before. They entertained one another from dusk 'til dawn. Marie finally realized that it was six in the morning, and she had to get going.

Just as soon as she got in, she managed to force herself to sleep, only to be awakened by Nancy yelling about her being out all night while her kids were hungry.

"Momma, I left them here with Shell! I know she fed my babies."

"That's beside the point. It's not our responsibility to keep your kids while you're out getting high with that junkie."

"Momma, I wasn't getting high!"

"You're a lie, and the truth is not in you," said Nancy.

"I know that was exactly why you didn't come home to take care of your kids."

Marie knew it too. She just didn't understand why Nancy had to call her out on it in front of everybody in the house. Nancy spoke like she was ashamed of her. Marie knew she couldn't keep listening to Nancy's put-downs. She also knew that she couldn't do what she wanted and not feel guilty about it, being in the same house with Nancy. She also couldn't tolerate Nancy undermining her when it came to disciplining her children.

"Hello," said a man with a baritone voice.

"Hey, baby, its Marie."

"Hey, my chocolate drop," Miller said. "How are you feeling after last night?"

"Oh, I was feeling pretty good until my mom cussed me out."

"Why did she do that?"

"She confronted me about being high and staying out."

"Oh my."

"Miller, I've had enough."

"Is there anything I can do for you?"

"Does your offer to move in still stand?"

"Yes. Anything for you."

"It will just be temporarily until my low income is ready."

"Sure, stay as long as you want," Miller reassured her.

Miller enjoyed having Marie and her children with him full time. It sort of made him feel like he was following in his parents' footsteps—that is, with him having the responsibility of raising and providing for a family and all.

He made sure that they were all settled in. His hopes were that Marie would enjoy the family life as much as he did and, therefore, decide to stay rather than leave once her apartment was available. He allowed her to decorate as she saw fit. She ironed and hung curtains in each room. She brought paintings and placed them all around the house to match the maroon-and-black color scheme.

He took her to Concord's department store and let her pick out anything Minnie Mouse to go in the girls' room. Not wanting to leave Lil' Man out, he chose a Batman sleeping bag for when he came on the weekends.

He desperately couldn't wait for his parents to meet Marie and the kids. He was just waiting on the perfect time to make that happen. He had been a little reluctant to because of how judgmental his mother, Edna, had become since she joined the Church of God and the Living.

He swore that she had joined a cult instead of a different denomination. Before she gave her life to the Lord and them, she tried to help anyone she could. She never talked bad about anyone. She felt that all people, no matter what their social background was, deserved to be treated fairly.

Edna was also at home taking care of the family more. They had always been her top priority. She very seldom visited anyone, unless they had a need. Somehow that had all changed.

One day, Edna received a phone call from one of her friends.

"Edna, you should come to my church revival on Wednesday night," Edna's friend Betty said. "Honey, I will tell you the truth, the Holy Ghost is going to fill the room!"

"What time does it start?"

"It's at 7:00 p.m."

"Oh, I don't get off until 6:00 p.m. that day. I won't have enough time to go home and get dressed."

"Oh, don't worry about that," Betty told Edna as she fanned her herself. "That's why I love that church so much—it's come as you are. They don't care what you're dressed in, as long as you're coming to praise the Lord!"

"Well, I will be there at 7:00 p.m."

Edna caught the Holy Ghost and gained a bunch of gossiping, judgmental church friends with it—at least, that's how he and his family viewed things.

That's why he wasn't going to introduce Marie to her until he was thoroughly convinced that she wouldn't be condemned or mistreated for being a single mother of three children out of wedlock. He knew all too well Edna's beliefs on that. He overheard her on the phone with one of her Holy Roller friends talking about another lady's niece getting knocked up by her boyfriend and now planning to move in together.

"Where are the girl's parents at? See, that's why these girls are getting themselves pregnant without a husband," Miller overheard Edna say.

"Their daddies aren't around."

He could tell that the lady on the other end of the phone agreed with Edna 100 percent.

"See, these girls need Jesus and an education, not a baby."

"They can barely take care of themselves. What a shame. What a shame. I know they'll all just end up on welfare."

He knew that the chances of her approving of his relationship with Marie were slim. His plan was to make some time to talk with his dad about it. He knew that his dad wouldn't be happy with his choice, but he was certain that he would support his decision. Miller was also hopeful that he could reason with Edna on the matter.

He decided to stay close to home and away from them as much as he could. He hadn't seen either in a month since he started dating Marie, mainly because of his guilt. Before Marie and the drug use, they had a great relationship. The lines of communication stayed open.

His dad had made several unannounced visits while Marie was home and Miller was working. Marie and the kids were naturals at playing possum when it came to unannounced company. She never opened the door.

Ignoring a knock at the door was almost a daily occurrence living with Nancy. Most times, it was a neighbor bumming sugar or a cigarette. Other times, it was the landlord trying to collect the rent. If Nancy didn't want to open the door, then the whole house learned very quickly the importance to remain silent.

Marie was uncomfortable with Miller's decision to ignore his parents. She felt that it was very disrespectful. She knew that his parents had to be worried. She had been there three weeks already, and they had come twice a week, only to get no response.

She often thought about her own family. She hadn't seen her mother or sisters since she moved out. They all had their opinions on why they felt that she was making another mistake.

She knew that Miller couldn't keep avoiding his parents.

"Baby, have you spoken to your parents yet?"

"No I haven't."

"They have to be worried sick about you."

"I'll take care of it baby," Miller assured, stroking Marie's cheek. "I am going to see my parents tomorrow."

His plan was to go and talk to them on Sunday. He would enjoy Sunday dinner with them and then tell them about Marie and the children. If that went well, then he'd try to muster up enough courage to ask for a loan.

Miller and Marie were heavy in their addiction. It seemed like all they wanted to do was get high and have sex—at least, that was all he wanted. He craved her body and loved her fluids. He could be at work and get aroused just from thinking about how good it felt being inside her vagina bareback. For her to have three children, it was still tight. Her muscles would grip his hard member with every stroke.

Once on the powder, everything seemed more intense for him. For her, it was different. She just wanted the high. The high caused her to go in another dimension. All her day-to-day problems didn't matter at all. She really didn't enjoy sex with Miller but knew the more she gave it to him, the more cocaine he brought. He'd buy an eight ball and that would last two days. They were to the point that they needed it around at all times. They would take care of the kids as best they could, but sometimes they couldn't get up.

"Momma, we are hungry," Starla said one day.

"Girl, go make ya'll some syrup-and-bread sandwiches. I think it's some more potato chips left. Split them too."

That became a frequent meal. Most times, there was plenty of food because of the food stamps that she received. She just didn't have the energy to cook.

Miller would try to be the head of the house. He would make sure that most of the bills were paid on time, but it was getting difficult to keep doing. His funds were depleting fast.

Before he met Marie, he was able to keep up all his appearances. He had enjoyed the fruits of his labor while also having enough to pay for all his necessities. He made over $65,000 a year at GM, so there was plenty of money coming in.

He was able to spend quite a bit on his drug habit that he had actually gotten during his college years at Wright State. He never saw any illegal drugs until then. He tried cocaine for the first time at a frat party to fit in.

He kept his addiction a secret to his family. He knew that they would be extremely hurt and angry. His being able to find a woman who didn't care about his shortcomings was all he ever wanted. When she confessed that she got high, he was elated.

Although he felt bad about not coming clean to her right away, he made up for it. She accepted his apology for keeping it from her and told him she understood why he did it. Now life was just the way he wanted it—at least, with having Marie and the kids around. He could finally be just plain ol' Miller. Around Marie, anyway.

"Hey, Mom. Hey, Dad." Miller found his parents in the kitchen.

His mother turned around from the stove with a pot of greens to face him.

"Where have you been, boy?"

His dad inquired as he stood up to walk over to him.

"Now hold on, honey, let him get in here good before you start all that," said Edna.

Edna was beautiful. She had a light complexion. She had small, feminine features and blue eyes. She was part black and part Muscogee Indian. She had long, jet-black hair that would wave up every time she added water to it. She was about five feet in height with a few extra pounds.

Miller Sr. was still handsome. He stood at six feet four and still had a firm physique. He had been an athlete his high school and college years, and it still showed. His hair, beard, and mustache were all covered in salt-and-pepper streaks. His lips matched those of Miller Jr., very full in nature. They fit perfectly on his chocolate skin tone.

After Miller hugged and kissed his parents, he set down to eat. Edna fixed meatloaf, mashed potatoes, greens, and homemade biscuits. She chose peach cobbler for dessert.

"Mom, Dad, I apologize for my absence. I have been busy with working and taking care of my family."

They were stunned.

"Your family! Are you married?" said Edna.

"You better explain yourself, boy," Said Miller Sr.

"Calm down, please. I am not married. I have been in a relationship with a woman named Marie. She is one of the greatest people that I know. We have decided to take our relationship a step further—"

"What does that mean?" Edna interrupted.

"We live together. She, I, and her children."

"She has children? Is she a divorced woman? Well, that means that she is an adulteress, and on top of that, she is committing fornication, living with a man out of wedlock!"

"How long have you been seeing this woman?" asked Miller Sr.

"Two months."

Miller Sr. just put his head down. He knew all too well when to speak and when to shut up. He knew that Edna would take it from there. It wasn't difficult for her to get to the bottom of things at all.

"Two months? Two months! You moved a complete stranger and her children in your home within two months of dating her? Have you lost your mind, son?"

"Mom, that's why I have been absent. I knew that you would judge us. I thought long and hard about this. Sin or not, I am going to ask that woman to be my wife."

"Over my dead body you are!"

Miller got up from the table, kissed his mom, and left.

"I don't believe in abortions or adoptions. What the hell has gotten into you? That is our baby you're talking about!" said Miller.

"I already have three kids out of wedlock," Marie said. "I don't want to bring another into the world without being married."

"I told you that we are going to get married. I just want my parents to accept it."

"That might not ever happen, Miller. They might never accept me or my kids. That's why I don't know if this is right."

Knock, knock.

Both of them stopped talking long enough for Miller to peek out of the closed curtain. He noticed it was Edna. He could tell that woman from a mile away. He jumped back from the window as quickly as he could.

"Who is it?" Marie asked.

"It's my mother."

"Well, aren't you going to let her in?"

Miller looked at Marie with a puzzled look. "Go. Let her in."

Edna was dressed in her nursing uniform. She looked very poised and professional. She decided that she would make a surprise visit after work. She hadn't seen her son since their last blowup. That hadn't set well with her at all. She loved her son dearly, and his absence had taken a toll on her and her husband.

Miller Sr. suggested that they allow Miller to be with whomever he loved. Rather, they felt like the woman was good enough or not didn't matter. What mattered was that their son was happy. She reluctantly agreed.

Now on the doorsteps of her son's apartment, she was hoping that he would allow her to come in to make things right.

Marie knew that that would be the day that his parents found out that she was eight months pregnant. There was no way she could hide it. At that moment, she'd wish that she and the kids would have been at her new apartment instead of letting it sit empty.

She was second-guessing her decision to stay put. After Miller's constant pleads to stay, she decided to keep her low-income apartment. She paid the rent but let it sit empty. She had one thing to be happy about—she and the kids were all cleaned up and well dressed. She had made it first priority to do so.

They were fully fed and tucked away in their room, playing with Barbie and Ken.

"Hello, my name is Edna," she said as she reached out her hand.

"Hi, my name is Marie."

Edna hadn't sat down yet before she started asking questions.

"Miller, is that yours?" Edna asked as she gazed at Marie's growing belly.

"Of course it is, Momma."

"How do you know?"

"Because I have been with her."

Marie couldn't believe what she was hearing. She wanted to tell his mother where to go, but she knew that would only make matters worse.

"Where are the other children?"

"Two are in the room playing, and her son is at home."

"At home? I thought this was home for them?"

"Mrs. Edna, my son lives with my great-aunt," Marie chimed in.

"Well, why doesn't he live with you? You had him."

"I am fully aware of that. However, we thought that would be the best decision."

"Who is *we*? Where is the daddy?"

"Mom, that's none of your business."

"Well, what my business is, is my grandbaby that she's carrying. I need to know all about that."

"Mom, she is eight months pregnant. They are both happy and healthy."

"Does it have everything it needs?"

"We have been picking things up here and there, but we still have work to do."

Edna looked at her son and saw a difference in his appearance. He looked thinner, and stress was all over his face. She felt so guilty. She felt responsible.

"Don't worry about getting anything else. I will get it everything it needs."

"Mom, we are having a girl."

Monica was born with cocaine in her system. Marie really didn't understand how. She stopped getting high a week before her due date. She thought that was more than enough time for it to be gone.

After Dr. Stevenson delivered the results, Miller walked out. He and Marie promised to quit getting high while she was pregnant. He had kept his promise; however, Marie had not.

Dr. Stevenson told her that he had no choice but to report his findings to child welfare services. He also contacted Nancy and told her all about what was going on. He knew that that was a breach in confidentially, but he knows that Marie was in big trouble.

Edna went in the room to talk to Marie. She had just left the nursery admiring her beautiful granddaughter. She was very upset with Marie but knew that scolding her for being a drug addict wasn't the best route to take.

"Marie, let me take care of her while you get yourself together," Edna offered.

Marie looked up at Edna with tears in her eyes and said, "I can't give my baby up."

"Marie, they are going to take her if you don't. At least she will still be with us. She will still be with her father. You can always see her whenever you want."

"Can you please go get Miller for me?" asked Marie.

Edna found Miller in the lobby talking to a woman she didn't recognize.

"Hey, Mom, I got someone I want you to meet. This is Marie's mom, Nancy. Nancy, this is my mother Edna."

"Pleased to meet you. Wish it was under better circumstances," said Edna.

"These are great circumstances. My grandbaby is in the world," Nancy replied. "Now somebody take me to my daughter."

Marie was relived but also ashamed to see her mother. She knew that it was a matter of time before Nancy would show up. Nancy reassured her daughter that they would get through all what was going on together. She promised that she would not let the white man take any of her grandkids. They would all be coming to stay with her until Marie got better.

Marie was overwhelmed with all of it. She wanted to see Miller and her baby.

Miller came in rocking Monica in his arms. He handed her to Marie. Marie looked at her beautiful daughter and sobbed. She knew that she had been wrong risking her daughter's life by getting high. She promised that she'd spend a lifetime trying to make it up.

She asked Miller to forgive her and not leave her.

Miller looked at her and said, "I do forgive you, but I have no choice but to leave. You could have killed our daughter. I think the best thing you can do is allow me and my family to raise her or we have no choice but to fight for full custody."

Marie allowed her baby to go with her father, and her two daughters went to live with Nancy. Marie went to rehab to get herself clean.

$$\text{————} \quad \text{12} \quad \text{————}$$

MARIE WAS FINALLY GOING home after a thirty-day stint in rehab. Nancy and her sisters were a strong support system while she was in rehab. They came every evening to the meetings. Each one got to share how Marie's drug abuse affected them all.

When Marie was released, her sisters were right there waiting for her. They told her that her low-income apartment was ready. They told her that Nancy was at the house with Lil' Man, Starla, and Harmony getting everything nice and tidy.

Dayton Metro Housing placed her in Arlington Courts. They were some projects that were on the south side of Dayton. Marie wasn't fond of either the area or her apartment, but she'd have to make do.

Marie was elated to see her mother and children. She was also glad to be in her own place. Though it only had three beds and a black-and-white television occupying the space, it was home—it was theirs.

While walking the girls to a corner store, Marie was stopped by a girl with copper skin wearing deep-red lipstick and an expensive-looking wig of blonde waves.

"Excuse me," said the street corner diva. "Do you have a light?"

Marie gave her a light for her cigarette. They stood on the corner and chatted as they smoked.

"Do you stay around the neighborhood? I'm not trying to be nosy, I just never seen you around before."

"Yes, I live in the Courts," admitted Marie.

"Girl, me too."

"What's your address?" Marie asked.

"It's 6543 Lily."

"I'm at the end, my address is 6553."

"Well, girl, my name is Cinnamon. If you ever need anything, knock."

"Thanks," Marie said. "I will."

Marie knew she wouldn't be knocking on anyone's door. She just had too much pride for that.

About a month later, Marie was looking through her cupboards and saw she didn't have anything for the girls to eat for breakfast, and her check had completely run out. She knew she couldn't possibly ask Nancy without her questioning why she didn't have food or money. She would eventually assume that drugs played a part.

She chose to ask Cinnamon instead. Soon after, Cinnamon proved that she was a good friend. If Marie didn't have food, Cinnamon would bring her food. If she didn't have cigarettes, she would bring them. If Cinnamon's favorite girls needed something, she would bring it. Marie grew to love Cinnamon like a big sister.

Lately Marie was starting to question how Cinnamon got all her money. She never seemed to go to work, but she never was broke. Marie would get her check on the first, and by the time she paid bills and got the girls something, her check would be almost gone. Definitely by the tenth, she would be broke.

She wasn't naive at all. She knew that Cinnamon was doing something illegal. She was convinced that it was drug dealing or prostitution.

One day, Cinnamon was over the house doing the girls' hair and hanging out. She and Marie sat at the table painting their nails.

"Girl, I need to ask you something," Marie finally asked.

Cinnamon perfected a French tip and looked up. "What's up, girl?"

"How do you keep money in your pocket? I can't do it. By the time I pay the bills from last month and get a few things for the girls, it is gone."

"Girl, I am a dancer," Cinnamon confessed.

"A dancer?" Marie asked.

"Yeah, I strip at a bar."

Marie pictured flashing lights, free drinks, dollar bills.

"So you make good money doing that?"

"Child, I make excellent money. I could bring home up to a hundred a night, just from dancing."

"Do you think I can get a job there?"

Dancing would be easy compared to walking the track. Marie still had her figure, and she knew how to use her body, especially if getting money was involved.

"I know you can," assured Cinnamon.

Marie and Cinnamon became inseparable. If you'd seen one, you'd see the other. They both worked at Fancy's Strip Club. Cinnamon was a dancer, and Marie was a bartender.

Marie had gotten back to her old self. Her beauty was back, and her purse was full.

Her family was coming to get the girls regularly, so she had a lot of free time. She and Cinnamon started dating some of the old men from the bar. They would tell those old men anything they wanted to hear, just to get their money. Marie had even managed to get the owner.

— ❈ 13 ❈ —

BY THE LATE SEVENTIES, crack had come on the scene. It was a moneymaker. This drug was better than cocaine and cheaper. You could cut cocaine with cheaper stuff like baking soda, and it would get you just as high or higher.

Cinnamon introduced Marie to this new high and to a life that she wasn't ready to live. Marie would fall in love with crack more than she had ever loved before.

Harmony soon came to learn her mother had chosen a drug over her.

She watched as Marie and her new boyfriend, Jake, screamed and fought. Sometimes Marie would take furniture out of the house, and it would never return. Starla and Harmony very seldom got to see Lil' Man or Monica. Hell, they barely got to see daylight.

They could never go outside to play. They had to ask permission to sit in "her" living room. Marie would tell them *yes* sometimes, but they had to sit on the floor. Their room was the only area they could be in, besides the bathroom or the kitchen, mainly because Marie and Jake were always entertaining guests.

Marie didn't play when it came to her house. She would make them clean and dust every day. Harmony felt that Marie hated them. Later, she would find out that Marie loved them more than life itself.

But when Harmony would be on her knees in the bathroom scrubbing at the toilet, she would ask her sister, "Starla, she hate us, don't she?"

Starla was older and had seen more. "No, Harmony, it's just that drug."

"What drug?" Harmony asked.

"Just forget about it, Harmony."

Harmony couldn't recall the day that she found out it was crack, but she could remember Starla and her snooping around in Marie's room when she and Jake were gone. They would find burned spoons, belts, and needles all in one spot. The scene looked very suspicious to both.

The first chance they got, they told their grandma. Nancy wasn't pleased by the news. She went off, calling Marie a junkie and anybody with whom she hung around were one too. She told the girls to hang in there and assured them that she'd take care of it.

Even still, it wasn't all bad times. The girls stayed with Marie and Jake for about two years. They were able to celebrate two Christmases and two birthdays. Marie and Jake laid them out for Christmas both years. Marie made sure they didn't go without on those special holidays.

Harmony later realized that Marie had been selling her body the whole time.

During those two years, Harmony's baby brother, Paul, was born. He was rarely home because Jake's side of the family wanted him to stay with them. Harmony missed him. She really had grown to love the little guy and felt like Marie was wrong for letting him leave all the time. Besides that, she and Starla never really got to go anywhere.

Jake and Marie would leave the kids at home a lot. When they would be home, they would stay stuck in their room.

Eventually, they were evicted for nonpayment of rent. Nancy allowed them to move in with her. Jake and Marie moved into her basement, and Starla and Harmony had to share a room. Harmony was so happy to finally be living with her grandmother again. She knew that she would be able to go outside and play. She also knew that Marie could no longer whoop her.

Nancy was a very spiritual woman. Harmony watched her pray all the time. She would wake up early Sunday morning and turn on *Bobby Jones Gospel*. She didn't go to church, but church would come to her.

The Jehovah's Witnesses would come and pray and study with her. Sometimes, Harmony would sit in. Before they moved in, Nancy didn't celebrate Christmas by giving gifts; but with them being there, she made an exception. Harmony loved her grandmother; she truly loved her.

Even while they lived in Nancy's basement, Marie and Jake were still getting high. Harmony and Starla would sometimes hear screaming and yelling coming from the basement and the sounds of furniture being thrown around.

Harmony never really knew why they fought, but they would often. Sometimes Marie would have to wear sunglasses in the winter because he would give her black eyes. Harmony hated him.

She felt like he was wrong for beating on her mother. She would later find out that those ass-kickings were often a result of something Marie did to the kids. Things between Jake and Harmony weren't the greatest at first, but the older she got, she learned to love and respect him for all that he had done for her.

Marie could steal and would. She would take stuff out the house and sell it. Things were so bad that she even took Harmony's brand-new bike and sold it. Jake beat her ass for it. He had bought it for Harmony.

Though all that was going on, it really didn't concern Harmony because she was with her grandmother. She knew that Nancy wouldn't let any harm come to her. Harmony was finally able to be a kid.

She could now go outside and play. She was such a tomboy! She liked playing football and climbing trees. She also loved to fight. She would beat boys up if they played too much. Even though she was a wild child, she hated getting dirty. She would change clothes at least twice a day. Marie and Nancy made sure she kept herself up right.

Nancy wouldn't sit back if her family was not groomed to perfection. She also didn't tolerate a dirty house or yard. She would make all the grandkids clean her house more than Marie had. Harmony never knew what cleaning a baseboard was until Nancy introduced her to it.

They would have to take all the curtains down and clean the windowsills. She hated weeds being along her fence and would make them go out there and pull them. But Harmony and Starla were used to cleaning from Marie, so they did everything Nancy asked. At least Nancy would let them have fun and invite friends over the house.

By this time, Starla and Harmony were both in high school. All the neighborhood boys and girls would come over to hang out. Starla was very popular; Harmony wasn't.

One guy who would come over and kick it was named Scott. He was about the only one who would pay Harmony some attention.

Starla couldn't stand him, and she let him know it. Whenever he came around, she would catch an instant attitude. She would sigh as she rolled her eyes. She strongly stated that she felt that he wanted to take her sister's innocence. That was a mission on every boy's mind in their neighborhood.

This Scott would tell Harmony how cute she was and how different she was from all the other girls with whom they went to school.

He would tell her things like, "You're going to be my wife when we get older."

"Over your dead body!" Starla would say.

He didn't care about her threat at all. He was determined to get what he wanted. He gave Harmony his number and told her to call him. Later, she would sneak and call.

They would sit on the phone and talk about everything. She would tell him how school went and how her mother was tripping out. He would tell her that things would get better. She believed him. She believed *in* him.

Things were getting a little serious with them. Harmony would sneak up to his house every day. They would sit in his room and listen to music. He would touch her in ways that were new to her. Certainly she knew about the birds and the bees—at least, that's what she told him.

Honestly, she did play house and "hide and go get it." So she figured that was sex. He would kiss her and sometimes try to go further.

She told him that she was still a virgin. He promised her that he would be the first to "introduce her to womanhood," as he would say. Harmony told him that's what she wanted.

They attempted, but it wasn't the right time.

Instead, they enjoyed lying there in each other's arms. Harmony enjoyed feeling like a real woman. It was just a great feeling knowing that someone cared.

$$\text{---}\ \text{14}\ \text{---}$$

Nancy was getting sick. She was diagnosed with lung cancer and had to be on oxygen. Harmony really didn't quite understand why all Nancy's long hair was falling out, but it was.

She was so used to Nancy sitting in her black recliner sipping her coffee while allowing Harmony to play with her hair, but now that was over. She no longer could take Harmony on the bus for their adventures. Nancy rarely smiled anymore. She just looked tired.

Harmony witnessed the strong woman she once knew become weak in strength, and she felt that she had no one to turn to. It was such a lonely time. Starla was hanging out with her new friends, Lil' Man was out on the streets, and Marie was out getting high with Jake. Harmony tried to sneak out and see Scott or talk to him on the phone, but she still felt alone.

One day she and Starla were in the hospital waiting for Nancy to finish getting her treatment. Harmony's stomach had been hurting for the last few days. She went to the bathroom to see if maybe that would help.

Sitting there in the stall, she looked down and almost shouted when she saw the blood in the toilet bowl. Harmony got so scared, she thought she was dying. She was afraid no one would tell Nancy goodbye for her and that Scott would be sad. Her heart started racing. She ran down the hall to grab Starla.

Harmony grabbed Starla and pulled her into the bathroom stall. She showed her what happened when she peed.

"Girl," Starla said, relieved and laughing. "You are becoming a woman! Get ready for this to happen every month."

Harmony was still in high school due to being held back twice. She had been praying that Nancy's cancer wouldn't take her away until she saw Harmony graduate high school. Harmony said all the prayers that she remembered from sitting at the table with her grandmother and the Jehovah's Witnesses. She prayed every time she saw the crosses on the corner-store churches and every night before she went to bed. He didn't answer.

One day, Nancy left her. Everyone in the neighborhood said that God had called for his angel to come home. While Nancy was celebrating in heaven, all of hell's angels broke loose on earth. Harmony's life would never be the same. It was now time for her to experience life without a protector and provider.

Aunts and uncles that rarely came over were now coming to take stuff out the house. The stuff that they didn't take, Marie had taken. Harmony saw Marie so upset and tried to comfort her mother. She couldn't. Marie was grieving, angry, and high.

The day of the funeral was so sad. Harmony didn't know what would happen to Starla and her. Marie was getting even higher and had been thrown out the house by her sisters Stacy and Tracy. They felt like she had to stand on her own two feet now.

Harmony spoke to Scott and told him she was thinking about running away after the funeral. He told her that she could come and live with him.

Soon after the funeral, she ran away. Scott's older sister was concerned that her family would call the police, so they hid her out over Scott's neighbors. Harmony didn't know that his sister had called and informed her family where she was.

The next day, Harmony was informed that she would be going to live with her aunt Stacy. Harmony didn't know her that well because her mother was so distant from everybody. She felt like this could work because Stacy seemed nice.

Harmony stayed with her for four months, and that was four months of hell for both of them. Harmony was still grieving the loss of Nancy. She couldn't focus, even though she wanted to do the right thing. She wanted to make Stacy proud, but she also longed for the life that she had just had to leave.

She couldn't see Scott. She didn't see her mother. She hadn't seen Starla. Stacy would tell Harmony what she expected from her. All she wanted was for her to go to school and get good grades.

Though Harmony had been an A student before, everything changed after Nancy's death. She wouldn't go or do the work when she did attend. She would act like she was going to school, and after Stacy left for work, Harmony would be right back home.

Her cousin Lexis was going through some of the same things that she was at the time. She and Harmony became very close. Harmony taught Lexis how to rebel against Stacy, the way she would with Marie.

The two girls were determined to show who the boss really was. The more that Stacy would try to lecture or punish Harmony, the more she looked at her aunt like she was the enemy. She wanted to be free.

It got so bad that Stacy would have to lock Harmony inside the house in order for her to stay put. She would take the phone so Harmony couldn't have any contact with the outside world. Harmony really felt like a prisoner. When Stacy would let her off punishment, Harmony would be right back in mischief.

At the age of eighteen, Harmony got involved with drugs. She started hanging out with older guys, and they would have weed and alcohol. She tried both and liked the way they made her feel. The feeling became a habit. Every day she was trying to hook up with somebody who had it.

Stacy found out that she was smoking in her house and called the police. After Harmony finished talking, they wanted to take

Stacy to jail for child neglect and abuse. Harmony told everything she could plus some. She found out that she was a good manipulator. It seemed she was truly her mother's daughter.

Eventually, Stacy had enough, and she beat Harmony with her fist. Once Harmony's aunt Shell heard about that, she came and got her.

Harmony liked living with her aunt Shell and her three sons. They were like her little brothers. Shell had a boyfriend who was living there also. He was funny. He was her favorite uncle. He would bring her all kinds of goodies and would tell everyone in the house, "Don't ask for any." He was very protective of Harmony—at least, that's what Harmony thought.

One night she was asleep downstairs on the couch. She was awakened by her uncle straddled on top of her with all his weight. She would later be violated.

Shell was stuck between believing her longtime lover or her troubled niece. Harmony had to leave.

When things didn't work at Shell's, Harmony moved back into Nancy's house. Harmony now was the queen of the castle. Starla and Lil' Man now lived there too.

Her aunt Tracy was now a great role model. She left the streets alone. She went and got a job at a nursing home. She would go to work often, leaving Lil' Man and Starla in charge. Harmony didn't mind that arrangement at all.

Harmony did whatever she wanted, as long as she was home before dark. She decided to get a haircut. She had been sporting a curl and wanted that thing gone. Tracy set her a hair appointment. Harmony had to catch the bus for the first time by herself. Tracy had given her instructions on how to get there and back.

Harmony got there and told the beautician exactly how she wanted her hair cut, "Cut it in stacks."

Harmony looked a little older with her new hairstyle. On her way home, she decided that she would not go all the way downtown to transfer bus routes. She knew that the bus she was on would take her close enough to just walk the rest of the way.

While she walked on Superior Street, she noticed a grey Cutlass with two guys staring at her. The one on the passenger side got out and walked into an apartment building, while the other drove off. As she approached the building, the guy came out to talk to her.

He was tall, dark, and fine. She would later say that it was love at first sight. She really felt a connection with him.

He came up to her as she was passing the steps.

"Hi," he smiled. "My name is Marco."

"I'm Harmony," she said shyly.

Marco was looking at her like she was the only person in the world.

"Can I get your number?"

She was thrilled.

"Yes."

Marco promised to give her time to get home before he would call. Harmony rushed home and stayed by the phone until he did. They talked for hours. She told him all about herself. He told her all about who he was and what he stood for. He told her that she was going to be his girl, no matter what.

The next day, she snuck to be with Marco. To Harmony, Marco was so real. He told her about how his mom had died and how he had to move in with his grandmother. She was strict, and Marco couldn't take that so he left.

He loved the streets, and the streets loved him. This boy was a hustler. He told her that he was working for somebody, but that would be short-lived. He couldn't keep working for just about anybody.

He believed in keeping his appearance up. He always had on a matching outfit with a hat and shoes to match. He also wore a big gold-link necklace with a matching bracelet.

Harmony and Marco were together every day. She told him all about her life, and he took care of her and hers. If she told him that her aunt Tracy didn't have money to get her hair done, he would spot them the cash.

Tracy would ask her how she got the money, and she'd say she found it. She wouldn't dare tell her aunt that she was getting taken care of by her protector and provider.

Marco had received a check because of his mother's passing. He got some smoker to take him and Harmony to the bank. Harmony sat in a chair and waited for him to take care of his business.

Soon she saw him walk over with a thick, white envelope. He sat down next to her and started counting a lot of money in front of her. He then reached over and handed her some money and told her to put it in her pocket.

"Harmony, whatever you need from now on, you come to me for it," Marco said, and she would do just that.

Word had gotten out that Harmony was messing with this twenty-nine-year-old man. Harmony was upset because she knew all hell would break loose. She had done her part by not telling, but Marco decided he wanted the streets to know they were together.

One night, she had spent the night over at a cousin's house and had forgotten to call Marco to tell him she wouldn't be home. By this time, she was officially Marco's "bitch." Though she was impressed by the title, she wasn't aware of what a position like that entailed.

It was considered an honor to be a man from the hood's bitch. Harmony was supposed to check in at all times but hadn't been schooled on that. She was about to learn what trouble that could cause.

Marco called the house late one night, and Lil' Man answered. By this time, he was a grown man. He too was in the game. He was known in the hood to not take any shit, especially when it came to his sisters.

"Hello, may I speak to Harmony?"

"Who is this?" said Lil' Man, instantly going into protection mode.

"This is Marco."

"Marco who?"

"Man, let me speak to my bitch."

"Who the hell is your bitch?"

"Harmony!"

"I'll beat your dumb ass. Don't call here looking for my eighteen-year-old sister."

"Eighteen?" yelled Marco.

"Yeah, she's eighteen."

"Man, I don't care how old she is, that's my girl, and we are going to be together. For real, you're her older brother, but I'm the one taking care of her," said Marco.

"What? You ain't doing shit!" replied Lil' Man.

"Who's been getting her hair done, fool?" asked Marco. "Who just put that hundred in her pocket? Me. I've been doing that."

Lil' Man ran in to Harmony's bedroom and woke her up in the middle of her sleep.

"Who is this fool that you been messing with?"

"I'm not messing with nobody," she lied.

"So why some dude named Marco call for you. He said that you were his bitch."

"Oh, I don't mess with him, he is just a friend," said Harmony.

"Well, tell me why this friend is giving you money? You got to be having sex with him."

"I am not having sex with nobody!"

Truth was, Harmony was a virgin. She had not yet experienced what having true sex was.

"He is not giving me any money," she added.

"Harmony, he said he has been getting your hair done and he gave you a hundred dollars."

"No he didn't. He gave me ten dollars, and I spent that earlier," she lied.

"Well, you can no longer see that punk-ass, period."

"Okay."

Harmony knew that Marco wouldn't want to mess with her anymore. She knew that he wouldn't dare be with an eighteen-year-old.

That next day, Lil' Man and his friends found out who Marco was and went to pay him a visit. Marco wasn't afraid of anybody.

"Man, I know that's your little sister," Marco said, telling Lil' Man up front. "I know that you love her, but so do I. I didn't know that she was just eighteen because she carries herself so much older. I just want you to know that I will not hurt her. I am not in this to get that pussy and run—I am in this for life. Hurting her is like hurting me. Whatever she need, I got it."

"Man, don't mistreat her or you're going have to see me," said Lil' Man.

Lil' Man went home and told Harmony that she was couldn't date anyone else. Marco would just have to be her first and last, so she'd better make this one work.

He was all too familiar with how easy a girl from the hood could get a bad reputation from being with several guys, and he didn't want that for his sisters.

Harmony called Marco and told him the good news. She was so happy that he still wanted to be her man. He told her that nothing could have kept them from being together, not even Lil' Man.

15

HER FIRST TIME WAS special. Marco had bought a radio and the soundtrack from *New Jack City*. He put in the cassette and laid her on the bed.

He started from her ears and worked his way down, teasing her with soft licks all over. The coolness of his breath teasing her skin drove her wild. She was so aroused. She begged him to explore her.

"Please," she whispered. "Come inside and feel my love."

"Not yet," he said, rubbing his fingers gently in a circle between her thighs. "Girl, you're not ready yet."

She moaned, aching for him.

"Not yet, I'll tell you when you're ready," Marco said.

He slipped his finger in her slowly, sliding it in and out gently, deeper and deeper. It felt so good. She begged him to believe her that she was ready. Finally, he gave the okay by getting on top of her, rubbing his tip over the opening to get her ready. She pressed back at him, hungering to feel his hardness inside her. She could feel pressure when he knocked at the entrance.

"You aight?" he whispered.

"Yes," Harmony whispered, wrapping her arms around his body. "I'm ready."

"I'll take it slow, baby," Marco promised.

He slipped in gently, moving deeper and deeper with each stroke.

The music was playing "(There You Go) Tellin' Me No" by Keith Sweat. Harmony, on the other hand, wasn't telling him no. She moved her hips to give him better access, gripping him as he gave her the pleasure that she craved. It was almost like he was moving to the beat of the drum.

"Damn, baby," he moaned quietly. "You feel so good."

He told her how much he loved her and how he always would. The way he said "I love you so much baby" echoed in her thoughts.

Afterward, they lay in bed together peacefully. She traced her fingers up and down his arm, telling him all the feelings that were in her heart. She wanted him to know how much she loved him and that she wanted to have his baby.

Marco promised they were doing life. Harmony would later experience what "doing life" really meant with Marco.

— 16 —

ONE NIGHT, THE HEAVYWEIGHT champion of the world Mike Tyson was to fight. He was Marco's favorite boxer. One of Marco's friends ordered the fight on cable. He called and told Harmony to be ready after the fight. He would pick her up after he watched it.

Being younger, she didn't know that there were several fights before the main event. She called him around 10:30 p.m. to see what was taking so long.

"Baby, the fight just started," Marco told her. "No sooner it's over, I'm coming, so be ready."

"I will be," Harmony replied.

Tyson won, and it was time to celebrate. Harmony knew the evening was going to go well. She put on her fitted jeans, a red-and-white Nike shirt, red-and-white shoes, and her red-and-white bra and panty set to match. She knew red made Marco go crazy.

All she could think about was her man. She wanted nothing more than to make him happy. She wished she could repay him for standing up for her. He was taking a little flak about her, but he didn't care. He would say, "Us against the world." A few years later, Tupac came out with a song about him being against the world, but that song was already familiar to her.

It helped having him around. So much was changing in Harmony's life, and it felt good to have Marco there to rely on. Things had gotten really bad at Tracy's, ever since she had snuck out the house to be with Marco.

Harmony thought that Tracy would be gone to work by the time he dropped her off from the Econo Lodge. It was hard to predict that Tracy would wake up that exhausted. She had decided to call off and relax around the house with the kids for a change. She cooked breakfast and woke everyone up but couldn't find Harmony.

They knew Harmony had snuck out when they searched her room and found her diary stating that she was going to be losing her virginity. Tracy was crushed. She felt that she wasn't home enough to monitor Harmony. She spoke to a close cousin of theirs named Tina.

Tina said that she was welcome over there. Tina was a hustler. She could sell drugs better than most, and that's just an understatement. She taught Harmony a little of the game like how to bag her socks up.

Tina took out the little plastic baggies and laid them out on the table, pointing to each one. "Harmony, this is a dime. This is a twenty, and this is a quarter."

Harmony had much respect for her. Marco had much respect for her too. With Tina and Marco on her side, she knew she would be all right. She was spoiled by both.

Harmony was also learning the game from both. Marco was selling crack. Harmony hung out with him and would watch him cook it. He would allow her to cut it into twenties and halves. He would give her the money and the gun to hide. She was his bitch. Harmony felt respected in her role.

Tina would allow Marco to spend the night. Harmony knew that many wouldn't have approved, but Tina knew that their relationship was special. One night, a man was shot and killed up the street from them. There were policemen everywhere. Harmony and Tina stood on the porch, trying to figure out what happened. The word on the street tried to say that Marco knew exactly what happened. Harmony defended her man as best she could.

The block was getting hot. The police was asking questions about Tina's house. She had turned her home into a full-blown drug house. If you wanted weed or pills, she had it; crack or cocaine,

Marco had it. The three of them had it worked out. If Tina or Marco had to make a run, Harmony was there to keep things moving.

She would answer the door, gun in hand, just like she was told to. She was respectful to all their customers, just like she was taught to do. Tina assured her that's what made them keep coming back. A lot of the other hustlers would mistreat their buyers because they had a habit. Tina and Marco believed in the old-school way of things—never kick anyone when they are down.

It was the first day of June, and they knew that business would be booming. They had extra on hand so they wouldn't run out. Tina told Harmony to not answer the door for anyone but regulars because they got word that some people were trying to rob them. She told Harmony to keep her gun on her at all times.

"Shoot if you have to and ask questions later," Tina told Harmony.

Harmony heard three knocks on the door. She grabbed the little .25 pistol that Tina had given her to carry for protection. She looked out the window and noticed one of their regulars named Joe.

"Hold on Joe." Harmony had to kick the two-by-four that served as extra protection from underneath the door before she could open it.

"What's up, girlfriend?" Joe said. "Can I get an eight ball?"

"Yeah, come on in," Harmony replied as she let their regular in.

Harmony couldn't help but wonder what happened to all his teeth. The last time she saw Joe, they were all there. Today was different. He had several that were broken. She dared not ask. Today, she was on a mission.

She weighed out the three grams on the little silver scale, put the coke in a plastic sandwich bag, and collected her ends.

She would later find out that Joe was an informant. Word had gotten out that a young chick was answering the door and serving. It was said that she showed the regulars more love. She knew that it was taking from her cut. However, she also knew in the long run it would pay off, if she ever started selling for herself.

After a good summer run, the police raided the house and carted Tina to jail and Harmony to children services. Marco went on the run. The police chose to not bring charges against Harmony. Her paperwork said that they considered her drug selling to be forced upon.

In Harmony's eyes, the only abusers were the cops who hit Tina in her head when she tried to flush all the dope in the toilet and the judge who sentenced Harmony to a group home once the nosy state asses got involved. The DA was so pissed off that the task force only managed to get some as evidence but never could recover the money. They knew there was a lot more.

With all the training the cops had, they didn't know the simplest rule: "If they are looking for something, put it right in their face." Thirty thousand was left in the dryer under the clothes.

In the detention center, a woman who addressed herself as Mrs. Hill told Harmony she was her caseworker. She assured Harmony she would now be treated well. She would now be safe from abuse. Harmony looked at the woman with total contempt.

She couldn't believe they were saying she was being abused. She knew full well that Tina and Marco loved her. As the woman kept talking, Harmony kept wondering where Marco was and if he knew what had gone on yet. She also wondered how much time Tina was looking at. Her thoughts stopped short long enough to hear the woman say Harmony was getting sent to live in Springfield.

"Where is Springfield?" asked Harmony.

Mrs. Hill told her that it was a city outside of Dayton. She told her that she would make certain that Harmony never had to see Tina and Marco again.

Harmony cried so hard; she hurt so badly. She was so scared. She couldn't believe what she was hearing. She felt lost. She couldn't imagine her life without Tina or Marco. Who would care for her? Who would protect her and teach her the rules of life?

— 17 —

THE GROUP HOME WAS nothing but a house that housed twenty girls. Most girls there were sentenced to stay until they were twenty-one. This was an alternative way of being in jail. They called it a group home, but there was nothing like home about it. They had wood bunk beds, and sometimes eight people shared a room. Two foster girls were lucky to have their own room. They were all given one locker to put their things in. If their things couldn't fit in the locker, then it would have to be bagged up and put in storage.

Every new girl got a list of all the dos and don'ts: Do make your bed up. Do clean up. Ask for permission to go back to your room to get whatever you had forgotten. Do ask to get something to drink. The kitchen and refrigerator were padlocked.

After thirty days of good behavior, you could earn the privilege of getting a pass outside, but it expired every hour. Every hour they had to stop whatever they were doing, go back to the house, sign in, and go back out. Every move was recorded by a staff woman. If she didn't like you, you'd know it by the write-ups she'd give you.

Allowance each month was thirty dollars. Every girl had to purchase their personal items with that—that is, if they wanted quality items. They could settle for what the state gave them or try to get what they needed another way. What the state issued to every girl wasn't good at all: A toothpaste that taste like fluoride. A toothbrush that processed frailty. A comb that would break, just as soon as a black girl tried to comb through their sometimes coarse hair. A bottle of lotion that was equivalent to water, and it never moisturized their skin. Lastly, a pack of Family Dollar sanitary napkins.

The only contact with the outside world was a payphone in the house. They never had quarters, so what the girls would do was call different calling card numbers and they would get the okay to place their call. It was so illegal, but they had no choice. There was one good thing though. The phone could receive incoming calls. The staff would make them take it off the hook at night.

Everybody in Springfield knew about the Plum Street group home girls. The new girls had a bad reputation passed down by the earlier bunch. They were all treated the same, and in many ways they were. When it came to street credibility, Harmony was no longer the most experienced. There were girls who knew and experienced way more. They were seasoned veterans when it came to having sex and stealing.

All her stuff would eventually be stolen. She had to learn survival skills quick. The staff would take them shopping with their thirty dollars, and she would see the clan stealing everything that wasn't nailed down.

Harmony had stolen once before, but she had gotten caught. She figured stealing wasn't for her. But as time went on, what Harmony lacked began to outweigh her fears. She too would pick up the survival instinct.

Harmony had been waiting by the phone for two weeks. No one called her. She didn't know if Marco or anyone even knew that she was still alive. And then one day, the phone rang!

"Harmony!" one of the girls shouted down the hallway.

Harmony was in her bed taking a nap, waking up every time the phone rang. When she heard her name being shouted, she jumped up and ran down the hall.

"It's a male," the young lady said, handing over the phone.

Harmony grabbed the phone and pressed it to her ear. Her heart was beating fast.

"Hello?"

"I'm coming to get you, baby," Marco's familiar voice came over the line.

Harmony burst into tears. She was speechless; all she could do was cry.

"Don't worry about anything. I am coming to get you, so have your stuff packed."

Harmony hung up the phone. She couldn't stop crying from relief. She wanted to be with Marco so bad and couldn't wait to get out of this house.

As the phone clicked back into the receiver, she sat back on the couch and let it all out. Everybody was looking at her crazy. She knew they thought she was lying about Marco. He never called, so they thought she had made Marco up.

Two days later, they were all sitting in their common area when there was a knock on the door. Harmony rushed up to answer it. Marco was standing on the porch.

"Go get your stuff, baby. I'm here to take you out of here."

The whole room went silent. Harmony held on to the doorframe to keep herself standing up. She was so relieved, her knees felt weak. She couldn't take her eyes off Marco's face. It took her a moment to think about what he said. How could she get her things and go?

"Marco, they won't let us go upstairs doing the day."

Marco looked out onto the curb where a running car was waiting for them. He looked back at Harmony and stroked her neck with a gentle touch. The look in his eyes gave her all the strength she needed.

"Don't worry about it," he said. "We'll go shopping."

Marco was hanging with a different person now. This guy was from Detroit. Detroit was known for being the go-to spot to get dope. It was better and cheaper there. Harmony didn't know how they had hooked up, but they were getting money.

Harmony and Marco decided to take a trip back to Dayton.

Marco told her to call and make a hair appointment. She did. Getting her hair done always did the trick. She left the shop feeling like a new woman, cleaner and lighter. She went back to the hotel where she and Marco were renting a room for a few nights. When she opened the door to their room, Marco was waiting for her with shopping bags full of gifts.

He laid each gift out on the bed and showed them to her. She counted at least seven matching outfits. She knew they had been stolen by some booster, but she didn't care.

"I love you, baby," Marco said. "No matter what happens."

That night, they made love over and over. The barest touch from Marco set her on fire—feeling his breath on her skin, hearing the small moans he made when she touched her tongue to him, the juiciness of his lower lip like a plump strawberry in her mouth, his broad hands roamed over the curves of her body. She felt every bit the new woman in his arms.

The first rays of the early-morning sun were peeking through the window by the time Harmony and Marco curled up together in the pile of sheets, resting and talking. Marco poured out his heart to her and told her everything he wanted for her life and his.

"Precious girl," he said, "if we ever have to part, please promise me something. I don't ever want you to be with nobody who don't love you as much as I do. Don't be with anybody who can't take care of you, mind, body, and soul. Understood?"

"I understand," whispered Harmony.

She closed her eyes and reached for Marco's hand, wrapping his fingers in hers.

❦ 18 ❦

Detroit was paranoid as hell. He constantly looked out windows and checked doors. He asked her a thousand and one questions about the group home. He asked Marco if he understood that he was harboring a runaway from a group home. He asked him if he knew how much time that carried for both of them, if caught. He was paranoid.

Harmony had been there about two weeks when Marco sat her down and told her that he would have to take her back. She understood. She didn't want him to get in trouble. He assured her that he would be moving to Springfield soon to be close to her.

She had to face the music. As punishment for leaving, she was on restriction for thirty days. This meant that she couldn't go outside and couldn't talk on the phone. The girls would give her messages from Marco. When the staff wasn't close, she would sneak to tell him she loved him.

Marco kept his word and moved to Springfield. He had hit a big lick and had to cut and run from Detroit. Harmony was glad he was close to her again, but she was also scared for Marco. The guy whom he robbed wasn't just going to settle for him leaving town.

Harmony was mad when he told her that he would have to move in with this girl from Springfield. She was hiding in the closet at 4:00 a.m., with the phone pulled in behind the door. She listened to Marco explain himself. A cold, sinking feeling took over her body.

"Harmony, I don't have a place to lay my head. If I keep staying at the hotel, I am going to spend all the money. If I stay with her and make her feel like I want her, then I can stay there, free of charge. It's only until I can find somebody to rent to me."

Harmony was too naive to understand that no one would rent to a known drug dealer and criminal. All she knew was that the man that she loved, the one who claimed to love her back, would be living with another woman.

She hung up the phone. She sat in the dark closet for a while, thinking about all that had happened. She decided what she needed to do next.

There was a guy named Tommy. He lived in the boys' group home. All the girls wanted him, but he wanted Harmony. She didn't throw herself on him, and he liked that. She knew he had a crush on her. Though her love was strong for Marco, she needed to teach him a lesson.

Marco moved in with the girl from Springfield. Harmony moved on with Tommy. Tommy was dark skinned with good hair and the whitest teeth ever. He also had the deepest dimples when he smiled. He asked Harmony why she was finally giving him a chance. She told him it was just time for her to move on.

She and Tommy spent every day together; either she was walking to his group home or he was walking to hers. He told her that he and his boy were about to get their own place and asked if she wanted to run away with him. She told him she'd think about it. Truth was, she wanted to see what Marco was going to do.

Tommy finally ran away and told her to come with him. She did. They stayed on the run for about month. Tommy had a few friends who let them sleep on the couch. They kicked it and ate cup noodles, hung out on the porch, and watched TV. It was good to be away from the group home rules and all the drama. Eventually, though, they had to make a move. Money was getting low.

Tommy wasn't about to let his girl believe that he wasn't a man. He knew that she was accustomed to nice things, and he was determined to keep that up. He and some friends decided to rob a store. Three left, but only Tommy came back. The other two were caught. Thankfully, neither one ever snitched on him.

One day, there was a knock on the door. Tommy stepped back for Harmony to answer.

Marco was waiting for her on the steps. She couldn't tell if he was pissed at her or just sad, probably a combination of both.

"I moved out," Marco said as he looked at her. "Now it's time for you to go back."

"I'll think about it," she replied.

Harmony didn't take long making up her mind. She knew that Tommy cared about her, but her love was with Marco. She went back to the group home and then was locked up. Because she was considered a legal resident of Dayton, she had to be transferred there to serve her twenty-day stay.

Tommy knew the protocol and wrote every day. She wondered why Marco hadn't.

After her stint in lockup, she was able to go back. One morning, she got a phone call. Picking up the line, she was shocked to hear the recording that it was a call from an inmate. It was Marco.

She needed to know everything.

"Are you okay?" she asked. "What happened? Why did you get locked up?"

"Harmony, when I found out you were living with that clown, I decided to move back to the motel. The same night, they raided the whole place and found my dope and my money."

Harmony was silent. She felt like this was all her fault. She told Marco how sorry she was for putting him through this. He told her that everything was okay. He knew she went with Tommy to get back at him.

"Ay, Harmony, they also wanted to question me about some murder in Dayton."

"What murder?" she asked.

"Do you remember the one that happened on the street where we lived with Tina?"

Just like that, her world had ended.

Despite her love interests thereafter, Harmony would never meet anyone else who could fill Marco's shoes. She would never meet anybody else who would show her what it meant to really love. In her quest, she tried to find what she had lost in many others, chasing a high called *love*.

She had to face the fact that she would never get the chance to sit back with Marco and watch their children play. He would never know how much he was treasured in her heart. She dreaded the fact that she would have to move on to what he once called "carbon copies of him." She felt that she would have to settle for what neither she nor he ever wanted for her.

He was charged with eighteen to life. After he told her the verdict, she poured out her heart to him. It was all she could give.

"I love you, Marco. I always will. Until death do us part. I thank you for showing me the kind of love that so many long for, and though I will not physically be doing time with you, spiritually I will. My soul will always ache for you."

$$\text{—— }\maltese\text{ 19 }\maltese\text{ ——}$$

Harmony hadn't heard from a family member in almost a year. She thought they had forgotten about her, until Tracy came bearing an outfit that she had purchased on behalf of Marie.

She caught Harmony up on everybody. Harmony told her about all the dos and don'ts they had to follow at the group home and how much she missed everyone back home. Tracy couldn't stay past six, and Harmony hated to see her go. She wanted so much to tell her that she was sorry for all the wrongs she had done. She wanted to ask for forgiveness for all her sins, known and unknown.

She wanted to say those things badly, but the words wouldn't come out.

Shortly after, Harmony was placed in another group home. This one was in Dayton. Harmony told her caseworker she had enough of the group homes. She asked could if she could find her a home, and she did.

Mrs. Dee was a God-fearing woman. She took Harmony in like she was one of her own. She knew her children couldn't stand Harmony, but that didn't matter. She made Harmony feel at home. Mrs. Dee lived in the same neighborhood that Harmony grew up in. Harmony was happy to be around the familiar streets and people in Dayton View.

Harmony was given her own room. She never had her own, so that was going to take some getting used to. Shortly after she moved in, another girl came in to Mrs. Dee's house. This girl was so pretty, with light skin and long hair. She had so much stuff. Harmony thought she had clothes, but that girl surpassed her.

"Harmony, meet Kelly," Mrs. Dee said. "She is going to be your roommate."

The girls hung out in their shared room and got to know each other. Harmony sat on the bed as she watched Kelly unpack all her clothes into the dresser.

Finally, I am no longer the youngest, Harmony thought. *I can teach her what I know.*

Little did she know, Kelly was fast! She would teach Harmony more than a thing or two.

Though Harmony had lived in the same neighborhood, she didn't stay in the same area as Kelly. Kelly grew up with her father who was also an ex-pimp. When her mother left, she forgot to take Kelly. That was her loss and his gain.

Kelly showed Harmony her report card, and she couldn't believe it. That girl was getting an A plus. Harmony made As but never an A plus. This girl was very smart. Who would ever know that it would take more than beauty and brains to survive a life like they were given?

Kelly told Harmony about street life. Harmony knew about dope dealers, but she never knew where they sold it. Marco made certain to not have her in the line of fire. Kelly told her about a street called Lexington.

It was around the corner from where they lived. Kelly's father also lived on that street. He was well into his sixties and couldn't handle her anymore. The street had a corner that was known as The Block. Truly, the name fit. The corner was alive all the time. It was a second home to drug dealers and a cornerstone for lost young girls who thought that they would one day meet their Prince Charming on that block.

Kelly and Harmony became two of those lost princesses. Every day they would get dressed in their best and walk down famous

Lexington Street. They would jump in cars with complete strangers, just because they looked harmless and had nice cars.

Though Harmony thought she was seasoned, Kelly would be the first to strike up a conversation. That girl could talk. Harmony would listen until she or the guy that they were with couldn't. She would later learn that though Kelly was prettier and book smart, she wasn't street smart like she was. Harmony couldn't remember who taught her the rule of speaking the fewest words, but she had mastered it.

Dealers started noticing them, and older guys in the neighborhood who watched the two girls grow up were getting eager. They would say how good they looked. There was a bet on who would get them.

Ray and Derrick were known drug dealers. They were popular, not only in their hood but to the city. Kelly and Harmony had major crushes on them. They would walk past the block, just to see if they'd notice them. They had.

One afternoon, Harmony and Kelly came past the block where Ray and Derrick were sitting. Kelly stopped to toss her long hair and put on some shiny pink lip gloss. Harmony gave them both a look and a smile and then looked away, pretending that she was watching the street too instead of sneaking glances at the guys.

"What's up, Kelly and Harmony?" Derrick nodded his head at the girls.

His eyes were half closed, like one of the street cats, but they could tell he was checking them out. Ray sat next to him on the steps. He had on a wifebeater that showed off his cut, lean arms. He leaned back on the steps like he owned them.

"Nothing," said Kelly.

"What's up with ya'll?" said Harmony.

"Shit. We're trying to kick it."

Harmony and Kelly looked at each other. Then Kelly turned back to the guys.

"When?"

"After, we finish hustling." Derrick looked down at the big gold watch on his wrist.

"All right, well just come to 200 Everett," said Ray.

Kelly flashed both the guys a smile and tossed her hair again. Harmony noticed a black tiger tattoo crawling up Ray's arm. She wondered if he had any other ones.

They rushed home to put on their sexiest clothes. They thought the outfits made them look older. Harmony put on a hot-pink spandex dress, with matching hot-pink hoops and bracelets. Kelly wore a red bra under a white tank top and jean shorts with the legs cut into a fringe. The pockets hung out so you could notice how short they were. The girls traded shoes and jewelry and makeup until they were happy with their final looks. Harmony learned to dress like that while living in the group home. Kelly learned from herself.

It took them more than two hours to get their outfits together. Shortly after dressing, they heard a horn. They tried to make the guys wait to prove to them they weren't pressed.

Out in the car, they nestled into their seats and their roles, Kelly in the front with Derrick and Harmony in the back with Ray.

"Hey, cutie," he said.

Harmony gave him a smile.

"I would like to formerly introduce myself. My name is Ray, what's yours?"

"Harmony."

"That's real pretty. I'd love to get to know you better, Harmony. Can we go out sometime?"

"Sure," she said with a grin

"Let's smoke this blunt," said Ray.

They rode around listening to music and getting high. They also decided to go to the drive-through and get them all a shorty of White Rose and Kool-Aid.

White Rose was a wine that didn't taste good by itself, but if you put Kool-Aid in it, you could stomach the taste. Harmony made hers taste like strawberry. She also made certain that bottle never left her hand.

Ray was so nice to Harmony. The guys asked them what they wanted to do. Both girls were used to guys who spent money on them. Harmony looked at Kelly and remembered how they both wanted their noses pierced.

"For real?" said Ray.

"Yeah, that'll be cute on you both," said Derrick.

They took them to the mall to get it done, and after that, they bought them matching outfits.

The guys would pick them up daily. They would take them to play miniature golf or go-kart racing. They would take them to the motel to kick it.

Word on the street was that both Ray and Derrick's exes wanted to hurt the young girls Ray and Derrick were messing with. Harmony and Kelly weren't worried at all. They felt that the girls were just mad because they stuck their men.

The girls lay across their beds talking while Harmony had to school Kelly when it came to not having sex too soon. She told her to make sure she got him before he got her. Kelly agreed.

Kelly came up with an idea.

"Girl, I think we should give them some now."

Harmony lifted her head up from reading her *Word Up!* magazine and looked in Kelly's direction.

"Girl, I was thinking the same thing earlier."

"I have been so horny."

"I am so tired of getting fingered in that back seat!" said Kelly. "I was so wet last night, I started to do it to him while we were sitting in the parking lot."

After much laughter, the girls called Derrick.

Derrick answered the phone with a blunt in his hand.

"What up, baby?"

"Hey, am I going to see you today?" Kelly asked.

"Yeah, you can see me. As long as you're not playing."

"What do you mean?"

"You know what I mean."

"No I don't!" said Kelly.

"I am tired of having blue balls. I ain't a little boy. I got needs…I can't keep playing around in the back seat."

"That's why I was calling you. Harmony and I would like to spend the night with ya'll."

Derrick nudged Ray who was sitting in the passenger side of the blue Cutlass.

He moved closer and put the phone up to both of their ears so Ray could hear what was being said.

"Where is Harmony?" Ray asked, whispering. "Is she trying to kick it with me like that?"

"Ain't gon be no fun if my boy can't have none," Derrick said.

"I told you, she's down with it!"

"Well, we will be there to swoop ya'll, just as soon as we hit these last three licks."

Kelly knew that meant—once they got through serving three customers.

"Okay. We will be waiting!"

They settled on the Dayton Motor Inn. It was a rundown motel off Dixie Drive. This was nothing like the places they tried to book a reservation for, but with it being Memorial Day weekend, they'd have to make do. Some of the building's white aluminum siding was missing. The siding that was left looked almost beige in color. Some of the numbers on the doors were painted on with a black marker.

The room had one full bed with a blanket that matched the curtains. Harmony decided to light her tea aroma candles for a sweet fresh scent. She went into the bathroom and freshened up. As she was putting on her pink matching lingerie set, Ray stood there looking at her.

She liked him even more. His great smile lit up the room. He was also well dressed. His slick black shirt was unbuttoned just a little to show a heavy gold chain around his neck. Ray was smitten as well. His sensitive spot started growing in his Guess jeans.

"Damn, baby. You are wearing that!" he said.

"You like?"

"Hell yeah, I like! Come on, baby. Let's go chill," he said.

Ray took a few puffs and passed the blunt to Harmony, who had settled on the bed. She made sure that she lay on her stomach, having him take notice of her ample bottom. She was so glad that they were finally alone. There were so many things that she wanted to say and show him how good he was to her.

She felt that he had been so patient with her. He would never get upset when she would tease him in the car. He would settle for her coming just close enough. However, tonight would be different. She would not keep her panties on to be safe.

The only teasing she would do was with her tongue. She licked him all over, from top to bottom. He grabbed her closer to him. He gripped her hips, and she straddled him, rubbing the wetness between her legs.

His hands would slide in and around the elastic as he reached to touch her, pressing his hardness against her. He taught her to rub her tenderest spot up and down while she rode him. He grabbed her by her waist, showing her the rhythm to take slow at first and then faster and faster until he came.

From that day forth, they were officially an item. When she got off work, it was about them. They would ride around the city listening to music and getting high. She would be with him while he handled business, and if he got pulled over, she would hold everything.

He would hand her his money to arrange and count. He would give her money and buy her clothes. She represented him; therefore, she had to dress in style. His favorite attire for her was anything leather and suede. He also paid for her hair and nails to get done.

She was now his partner in love and crime. Since Derrick wasn't around any longer, Derrick went back to his older girlfriend after she gave him an ultimatum. She told him that either he left young Kelly completely alone or she'd report his ass to the cops.

Harmony knew that Kelly really cared about him a lot. She reassured her that he only left because of the threat of going back to prison. He knew with a statutory rape charge, he'd be there for a long time.

Kelly was getting jealous because she barely saw Harmony, except for curfew. She also didn't like all the new gifts she was getting without her benefitting. Harmony didn't mean any harm, but they didn't have much in common lately. She took Kelly with her and Ray as much as she could. For Kelly, it was never enough. Harmony also managed to buy Kelly an outfit or two, just so she wouldn't feel too left out. All Kelly wanted was her best friend back.

Ray wasn't having that. He thought Kelly was a loudmouth and too promiscuous.

"I know that's your foster sister, but ever since she and Derrick cooled off, she has been going from guy to guy," Ray told Harmony. "She is getting a bad reputation out here. I need you to distance yourself from her."

Harmony listened to him and did just that. She didn't want a bad reputation. She also didn't want to lose what she had.

Ray was good guy. He didn't want to sell drugs but had no other choice. He told her that their relationship could only work if she went to school. He told her that he'd pick her up and take her to school. Harmony also got a job at McDonald's, and he promised to take her there also.

In a lot of ways, he reminded her of Marco. That was why she fell for him so hard. Every day, Ray kept his promise. He would drop her off at home around her curfew time.

For a while, she thought she was his one and only, but Ray was slick. Harmony found out that he lied about his age and about him being the father of two kids. He stuck to his lie, until she found out about his kids' mother.

One day while picking Harmony up from work, Ray had to stop and use the bathroom. Harmony was looking around the inside of the car and saw a letter with flowers all over it. She took the letter out and started reading it. It was from his woman and the mother of his children. She had written to thank him for the kids' Christmas. She apologized for stealing all his drugs. She told him that she loved him and couldn't wait to be with him when she got home.

Harmony was hurt. She didn't understand how Ray could have fooled her for almost five months. As soon as he sat down in the car, she slapped him. He grabbed her arms and asked her why she just did that. Harmony told him she knew everything. She confessed to reading the letter. He told her that he was sorry he lied and that it would never happen again.

Ray told her all about his ex, how she was in rehab and how she had done so much that he couldn't forgive. He told Harmony that he only wanted her and that he was in love with her.

$$\text{20}$$

Harmony found out she was pregnant on her birthday. Her sister Starla had bought her a cake and balloons. She decided what better time to deliver the news. Starla was excited and told her to keep it.

Harmony wanted to badly but didn't think Ray would be happy about it. She knew that their relationship wasn't in a healthy place at the time. He would later prove her right by moving on to others.

She couldn't believe that he was playing her while she was carrying his seed. She would catch him messing with girls younger than her and girls who were older than him. He was just wild.

Harmony was so depressed. She had never had a guy play her like Ray was doing. She tried to do everything she could to make him love her again. Nothing worked. She cried every day. She knew that she was stressing the baby, but more so, she was also stressed.

Harmony would pray and ask God to help her relationship. She really wanted to start a family with Ray. She knew that he could be a good father to their baby, the same way he was to his others. Harmony didn't hear from God fast enough. She decided to end it.

Ray tried to talk her out of it, but she had made up her mind. He paid for it and told her the blood was on her hands. She endured that experience, with nobody there to hold her hand. She did it alone.

No sooner than she had healed, Ray was right back chasing after her. Harmony would later come to understand why. She felt that Ray had her right where he wanted her when she was pregnant. He felt that he stood a better chance of not losing her if she had his child. They would be committed for life—well, at least, she would be.

When she had the abortion, he felt that she was also trying to leave him. He was absolutely right. Harmony was finished. It was time to show him who she was.

She made him chase her all over Dayton. She would ignore his phone calls, and when she decided to be bothered with him, she made certain he cashed her out. She set out to meet new acquaintances. She wanted to be up on all the latest events. She even got herself a new friend.

Tiffany was just what Harmony needed. She was cute and about the same size as Harmony. Their styles matched. They shared so much in common, both even came from broken homes. Though Tiffany still lived at home, her home life was far from perfect.

Tiffany's mother beat her. Each time it happened, Tiffany would run away, and Harmony would sneak her into her foster home. Tiffany was Harmony's girl. They talked about everything. Harmony had never trusted a female as much as she did Tiffany. She'd hope that Tiffany would never betray her.

However, Ray hated Tiffany. He really hated anybody who would be an outlet for Harmony. He couldn't stand that she and Tiffany would hang every day. They both would get dressed up and walk the streets, trying to find some action. They would find plenty of it.

Harmony paid less attention to Ray and more to Tiffany, her new friend. Though she was seeing other people, Ray was still a part of her life. They still fought and made love. She felt connected to Ray. She would talk to him about the abortion. She would share with him how she wished that they could make things work. She would even ask him what she could do to make their lovemaking better. She wanted to please him so much that he wouldn't want anyone else.

He told her how crack was an aphrodisiac, how he had witnessed female geekers use it and then have the wildest sex. He made her feel like that was why he would choose his kid's mother over her. She didn't know if alcohol was the reason why he introduced her to a "cigamo," but that high almost cost her, her life. A cigamo was like a joint, but instead of marijuana, it was crack and tobacco mixed. She took a puff of it and was high. She told him she had had enough.

After lying down for the evening, she prayed herself to sleep and vowed that that would be the first and last time she ever tried that. Somehow, she managed to go to sleep. When she woke up the next morning, she made it a point to keep busy. She figured if she stayed focused on different things about the day, she wouldn't have time to be trying to chase a high.

She also tried avoiding Ray's phone calls. She felt he tried to kill her. He assured her he did not. He told her how much he loved her and how he wanted to spend the rest of his life with her. The things he told her were nothing new, but she wanted so bad to believe him this time.

He told her about his plan to move out on his own. He promised her he wanted her to move in with him. The day that it was supposed to happen came and went.

Ray was enjoying his newfound freedom—one that consisted of sex, drugs, and money. Harmony had had enough. She had called him so many times with different women in that apartment. She decided to leave him for good.

She didn't know anything about Tennessee, but a girl that she knew did. Harmony needed money to get there. It didn't take long for her to figure out a way to get some. She broke into Ray's apartment while he was asleep. She took his money, his jewelry, his dope, and his keys. She then decided to take the car.

Ray was so drunk, he hadn't heard or felt anything. Harmony called Starla and told her what she had done. Harmony told her that she needed her to follow her and return Ray's car. Starla agreed. Once they got to the bus station, Starla said she thought Harmony should call and say goodbye to him. Harmony should have known that that would be a mistake.

She called him from a pay phone outside the bus station. As the phone rang, she looked down at the big duffel bag at her feet full of dope, money, and jewelry.

Ray picked up on the other line. He sounded like he was still drunk and barely awake.

"Hello," said Harmony.

"Harmony," Ray slurred. "Baby, please bring me back my stuff."

"I just called to say goodbye," she assured him.

"Goodbye? What you mean?"

"I'm moving to Tennessee."

"Baby, please don't leave me, let's talk this out," he begged. "I'll change, I promise."

Against her better judgment, she believed him yet again. Starla drove her back to Ray's house. He changed for a month.

Harmony and Ray's fights caused another eviction for Harmony. She had been staying in two different foster homes, although both were unfit. Despite the homes getting the max amount of money allowed for her, she didn't have a bed to sleep in. She had to sleep on the floor. She and the other foster girls would go without food or even sanitary napkins. Once she had to use a baby diaper.

She couldn't take those conditions anymore. She reported child services to the *Dayton Daily News*. She also protested in front of child services with a sign that read, "Lord, please hear our prayer. We need decent people to come forth and care for us." On the back it read, "No peace unto the wicked." She was shipped off to a residential treatment facility located in Columbus, Ohio, the next day.

In Columbus, she couldn't use the phone at all. She was escorted everywhere until she earned their trust. She was different from the teens who were there. She didn't belong. The nuns knew she didn't. They moved her to their group home.

Being at the group home with the nuns taught her so much. She decided she didn't want to take life for granted. She knew that she couldn't depend on any man to give her all she needed. She decided to get a job. The nuns made sure that she put half her check in savings.

She even joined a program called "Reach Back." It was designed to help at-risk teens. They would have group sessions about peer pressure, sex education, drug and alcohol prevention, and grief counseling, since a lot of the teens came from broken homes.

As part of her work with Reach Back, Harmony went to a convention in Bowling Green, Ohio, with teens from all over the state.

Standing there in the crowded room, all of a sudden, she heard someone say, "Leather Puss!"

It was someone from her school in Dayton. Memories of her old life with Ray came rushing back. She rolled her eyes and walked away.

21

Harmony's birthday was on its way, and she had nothing to show for it. By now, she was living in the projects on Mound Street with her girl Shannon whom she had met through Reach Back.

She decided she needed to do something with her life and went to sign up for Job Corps. They shipped her to Detroit. She stayed there for six months, long enough to receive her GED, but was kicked out soon after. They gave her a bus ticket back to Mound Street.

Shannon was glad Harmony was home. She had given birth to Harmony's goddaughter, and she missed having her around. Harmony knew that she would have to make up for the lost time.

There was a temp service up the street. Harmony went in there to fill out an application. She got hired for two jobs right on the spot. By day, she was responsible for cleaning bathrooms at a convention center; during the evening, she would assist the owner of the temp service with his inadequacy. In return, he promised to pay her well for both jobs.

Mr. Hall was an older man who once marched with Martin Luther King Jr. He was well into his sixties but wanted Harmony to make him feel like he wasn't. He could no longer achieve an erection but still wanted to feel like a man.

"Sweet face, you don't belong over here," he would say.

That was something Harmony already knew. He told her to find a place and he'd pay half of everything. She wasted no time, and she found a place in a week.

Mr. Hall also spoke to the supervisor at the convention center and got her a full-time position. Harmony couldn't have been happier. Not only did she get a check from the convention center, she also got one taking care of Mr. Hall when he needed. Two checks a week wasn't bad. It wasn't bad at all.

With Harmony's newfound wealth came newfound friends. Not being naive to why many wanted to be around her, she chose her friends wisely. She was introduced to a young guy named Dia. Though Dia was born a male, there would prove to be nothing male about him.

Harmony had never seen a transsexual before—that is, until she met Dia. Dia was eighteen but looked much older. She was six feet one in height, with thick-boned curves, just like a woman. A beautiful woman at that. Her smile would light up a room. She had golden skin with very fine feminine features. Harmony was mesmerized by Dia's attitude and grace. She walked like a woman, spoke like one, and laughed like one. She couldn't believe that Dia was born that way.

Indeed, to Harmony, Dia was all woman. She could put on makeup better than most women she knew. She could also do hair. She loved trying new hairstyles on Harmony. Frankly, there wasn't too much that Dia couldn't do. She could sing, dance, and impersonate. On nights that they decided to stay home, she enjoyed his comedy skits. She had a new running buddy and roommate.

She and Dia would do everything together. They enjoyed going to rap concerts and watching old movies. They would sit up for hours and talk. To Harmony, Dia was her student, and she was going to teach her how to survive. Dia's parents were in jail. Harmony had spoken to her mom several times and had promised her she would look after Dia until she came home. She did.

Dia was very outspoken until it came to her sexuality. She would keep that a secret. Harmony knew that she was playing a dirty game when it came to her not telling guys that she was born male, but who was she to judge? Harmony continued to work hard and had gotten herself a car. She would later have to escort in order to keep that Ford Escort.

Harmony and Dia both indulged in powder in the past. It was an experience they both had before they met. Harmony told Dia that it was something that neither one would be doing anymore. She had quit, but Dia had not. They partied hard. Having to foot the bill for everything put a strain on Harmony. She wasn't used to taking care of anybody like that. She sat Dia down and told her that she needed a job. She got one as a shampoo assistant.

Harmony lost her job due to cutbacks. She knew she had no other choice. She called Mr. Hall. She explained to him what was going on. He told her to come back and work for his temp service.

Though she was grateful to have an income, the jobs were grossing her out by the day. Mr. Hall was also getting sick and could no longer fake having an orgasm. The money that she normally received from him was nonexistent. Harmony began to stress out over money. She was about to miss a car payment and needed some money quick. She had no one from whom she could borrow three hundred dollars.

While looking in the newspaper she read an ad that said, "Models needed! All shapes and sizes, for an escort service. Pay up to $2000.00 weekly!"

Harmony called the number and spoke to a woman with a very raspy voice. She asked Harmony her name, height, weight, and then her age.

"Nineteen," Harmony told her.

She then asked when Harmony could start.

"ASAP," Harmony said.

Harmony always dreamed about becoming a model.

She pulled up to a house on Valley Street that seemed like a mansion to her. She looked down at her directions to doubl- check the address, "550 Valley Street." That was the place for her job interview.

Harmony couldn't wait to get inside that house. She had always wanted to see how black people lived out there in Dublin. She rang the bell and was greeted by a butler—or, at least, that's what she thought he was. Turns out, he was the husband to the head lady in charge.

"Ms. Stephanie will be right with you," he said to Harmony, asking her sit in the foyer to wait.

Harmony sat patiently, admiring all the paintings and beautiful furniture in the foyer. She loved the open bay windows and the high ceilings. The house had windows everywhere, and the sun put them to good use.

After a few minutes, a tall, beautiful woman approached her.

"Hello," she said. "My name is Ms. Stephanie."

With her hair swept back into a high bun and a perfect pearl necklace caressing her throat, she looked every bit the successful businesswoman.

Harmony stood and introduced herself.

"Hi, I am Harmony."

Ms. Stephanie gave Harmony an approving look from head to toe. She nodded her head and waved in the direction of a long hallway.

"Please follow me," she said, taking Harmony to her office.

The room they entered was as polished as the rest of the house, with plush carpeting and leather chairs next to a very well-organized desk. Ms. Stephanie gestured toward one of the chairs, and Harmony sat down. Stephanie sat behind the desk and looked hard at Harmony.

"Well," she said, "I am quite pleased with your appearance. You are a lovely-looking young lady."

Harmony was very proud.

"Thank you," she replied. "It is a pleasure to visit your home, it's simply beautiful."

She told Harmony that her job was to provide a man with company. She said that she had contacts with some very rich men who were often looking for models or companions. The men would pay

Harmony for her time, and in return, she would pay Ms. Stephanie for making the business connection.

"We work mainly with white-collar businessmen, doctors, lawyers," Ms. Stephanie explained. "Often they are just lonely single men looking for companionship. Of course, what two consenting adults want to do is their business. All we provide is the connection for the customer to have the company of a woman."

As Ms. Stephanie continued, Harmony got the point that most girls who didn't have sex didn't get many requests. Eventually, they got down to discussing money. Ms. Stephanie told her that if she ever wanted to charge her customer for extra services, she should charge $180. Ms. Stephanie would get $50 and the driver $20, which would leave Harmony with $110. If for any reason the customer wanted her to stay with him all night, then the clock stopped at $600.

When Ms. started describing the trips that some of her clients had taken her and some of her girls on, Harmony thought about all the places that she wanted to visit on someone else's dime like Paris or Las Vegas, to name a few. Ms. Stephanie was big on her girls protecting themselves, if they decided to have sexual intercourse. She told Harmony that if she were to ever decide that she wanted to have sex, even though she was not running a prostitution ring, she still suggested to Harmony she use condoms.

She also needed for her to go down to the health department and get a complete physical and bring her back the results to ensure safety. She informed Harmony that she would need to see new results every six months.

"If you decide to stick around that long," Ms. Stephanie added.

Ms. Stephanie was crazy. She thought Harmony was going to work day and night. Harmony was content with what she was getting. Her rent was $295 a month. She paid it up. She was cool with a job here, a job there; Ms. Stephanie, on the other hand, wasn't. She knew Harmony's potential. She knew that she could go a long way in the business. She hated that Harmony didn't love money as much as she did.

Ms. Stephanie would call and wake up Harmony out of her sleep. Harmony would tell her she wasn't going. She would beg Harmony or would promise to lower her fee. Harmony had to go on call after call. Some wanted conversation; some wanted extra attention.

Phat Daddy, her driver, was part of the reason why she didn't want to go. She had heard about people falling asleep behind the wheel of a car, but she had never driven with one—that is, until she climbed into Phat Daddy's van. Mostly, all her calls were in the suburbs, a long way from home. They would be riding and talking one minute, and the next, he'd be snoring. She would have to steer while waking him up. She calculated that she had had too many near-death experiences within a week's time.

She quit. Harmony only lasted two weeks.

After a week of sitting around not making any money and being annoyed by Ms. Stephanie calling day in day out, she came up with the perfect plan. She would take this much-needed break in order for her regulars to miss her. She would then come back to work for Ms. Stephanie for a brief moment until she could give her regulars her number. She would also make her regulars think that they were getting a deal.

Their new price will be $160. She would be saving them twenty and was gaining thirty. After giving a driver his twenty for gas and protection, she would make a killing. Off to work she went.

After three months, she had enough. She could no longer sell her body or the bodies of the ladies that she recruited. Somehow, she thought that money would be the answer to all her problems but learned that wasn't the case.

Giving her body with no love or commitment only drove her self-esteem low. She never thought that she would have to result to such measures in order to survive. It was a life that neither she nor God wanted her to live. She wanted to take her life. She thought about all the ways she could do it.

She almost swallowed a whole bottle of pills with a pint of vodka. But as she was about to, she heard a small voice say, *"Get down on your knees and pray."*

She prayed so hard that she could feel God's presence resting on her. She vowed to get anything that wasn't of him out of her life. She prayed he would forgive her for all that she had done.

The next day, she got up and went to get a newspaper. As she was flipping through the classifieds, an ad caught her eye:

> CNA classes now, being held! Do you like helping people? Are you twenty years or older? Come join our team at West Pointe Nursing Home. We pay for training.

She called the number on the ad and never looked back.

She worked so hard. She put everything she had into nursing. She knew she wanted more and was determined to get it. She had vowed to never again use her body to get anywhere, but instead, she would use the mind that God gave her. She would work to get what was rightfully hers.

On her path to a better life, she did stumble a few times. Her strength was in knowing that God was on her side. She decided that it would be best if she found a church that was after God's heart as much as she was.

She found one at the Greater Blessing Apostolic Church. Bishop Tate was a God-fearing man. He read from the Bible and sometimes had a word straight from God. He would call people to the altar to pray for them, and sometimes he would tell them what God told him to tell them.

After the people would hear the message, they would scream, cry, jump up and down, or take off running. Sister Elsie would do all the above. At first, Harmony thought that it was strange. Then one day, she too had an experience with the Holy Spirit.

It was four Sundays after her initial visit. Harmony joined the fellowship and was quickly a candidate for baptism. She knew that God was calling her for a greater purpose. Bishop Tate told her that God sees all, that she had to endure growing up, and that the battle was no longer hers but the Lord's. She no longer had to fight by herself because God Almighty was her Protector and Provider from that day forth.

Harmony felt that Bishop Tate knew all her secrets—although, luckily, he did not put all her business out on Front Street. When she first felt the true power of the church and God's love, she cried so hard. She thanked God for answering all her prayers. She was relieved that he was now on his way to rescue her from all hurt, harm, and danger.

She told Bishop Tate that she wanted to give her life to Christ. He told her of God's word and that she would be saved. He also told her that she needed to be washed and made whole.

He told her that she would go down in the water a sinner but come up from it born again. She would be a new person. All her sins would be washed away. She agreed to be baptized the following Sunday in front of the whole congregation.

Harmony was excited and fearful about the baptism. She was excited to know that all her sins would be forgiven by God. She thought about her abortion. She thought about all the sex that she had and not being married. She thought about the lies she sometimes told. But all those sins would be forgiven.

She then began to think about the fact that she couldn't swim. She wondered how long she had to stay under water. She hoped the time wasn't measured by all the sins she had committed. Certainly she wouldn't make it out of there alive if that were so.

She prayed more than ever. She wanted a close relationship with him and knew that prayer was the path. She asked that he keep his promise to forgive her. She asked him to send positive people to her—no more drug dealers and no more sinners who enjoyed their sinful lifestyles.

She wanted a new life.

The first Sunday each month was a special day. It was the day that the church took communion and held baptisms. Harmony was the only one who was a candidate for the baptism on that first Sunday, so the bishop took more time than usual on her. He told of the story of the woman with the issue of blood and how Jesus healed her.

"Though, Sister Harmony, that is not your case, thus saith the Lord, 'Your issue of sin has been great. I have seen all that you have done in secret. I have seen all that has been done in public. Though man may not forgive, yet I forgive you. I am your God.'

"'From your mother's womb, I knew you. When all deserted you, it was I who came past and covered your nakedness. It was I who fed you when you were hungry. Though you've felt that you've been alone, you haven't. I've been right there. I forgive you, my daughter.'"

He then dipped her in the water and bought her back up, saying, "In the name of the Father, the Son, and the Holy Spirit."

Everyone cheered; some even shouted, ran, or jumped in celebration.

Harmony didn't understand what all the fuss over her was about. It hadn't dawned on her that even the angels in heaven were cheering. She didn't understand the real significance of it all, not until she grew in her walk with Christ.

$$\text{—}\!\!\!\text{—} \quad 22 \quad \text{—}\!\!\!\text{—}$$

Living life on the right side of the road proved to be difficult for Harmony. With all her friends gone, she felt a void. She reached out and made contact with the family who had abandoned her.

She knew that part of her vow to serve God meant she would have to make peace. She called everybody that she had lived with and thanked them. She also apologized for all the hell she had caused. After apologies were made, she felt it was time to get to know them.

Marie had called and asked if she could stay with Harmony. Harmony felt like that would be an opportunity for her to build a relationship with her mother. She agreed.

Marie had been living in Lexington, Kentucky. She had decided to move there to get herself clean. That move had proven to not go so well. She expressed to Harmony how years of drug abuse had taken its toll on her. Harmony felt so bad for her. She wanted to help Marie finally kick her habit.

Before she set out to make the arrangements, she took a minute to reflect on the goodness of God. She was thankful that he had not allowed her cocaine or heroin use get the best of her. Though she had sampled both on many occasions, she never got addicted. She had loved the way heroin made her feel and therefore knew that she had to stay away from it.

Harmony was no longer naive. She knew that it wasn't her strength alone that kept her away but the strength of her Creator. Sometimes she wondered what was so special about her.

Why did He choose to spare me when countless numbers of my friends had gotten hooked? Harmony wondered.

She had lost a foster sister, and her best friend Deon. Instead of questioning God, she thanked him for sparing her.

After completing all the arrangements for Marie to come, she set out to work. West Pointe was not an easy nursing home to work for. Harmony had been there eight months and had the pleasure of knowing two administrators and two directors of nursing. West Pointe was the worst. The only reason why Harmony stayed was the pay and the love for her residents. She enjoyed talking to the elderly, for she knew they held much wisdom.

On breaks, she would camp out in their room and have them take her down their memory lane. They would tell her everything.

Mr. Bob told her how he had cheated on his wife for many years and how she never found out before she passed away. Instead of him being happy that he never got caught, he was sad—sad because he never got the chance to confess his sins to her. Harmony wondered why that was such a big deal to him. She even committed plenty of sins she hadn't told anyone about. Why would exposing them make her feel any better?

Tuesday morning, she woke up earlier than her usual five o'clock alarm. She was nervous about seeing her mom. She hadn't laid eyes on her mother in years.

Harmony picked Marie up from the Greyhound bus station. She hadn't seen her mother in almost three years and really was excited. As the bus unloaded, she searched long and hard for the woman she remembered. Her search went cold.

Many thoughts raced through Harmony's mind.

Did she not show up? Harmony thought. *Why would she have me go through all this trouble if she wasn't going to come?"*

Suddenly, Harmony noticed a thin, frail woman waving her arms in the crowd.

"Hey, baby!"

Marie weighed barely a hundred pounds and was in bad shape.

Harmony ran to meet the woman she once knew. She threw her arms around her mother's decaying structure.

"Come on, Mom. I am going to take care of you."

On the ride home, they caught up on all the current events.

Marie told her that she and Jake were no longer together and how she just wanted to focus on getting sober.

"I'm so ashamed for you to see me like this," she told her daughter. "But I really need your help, baby."

Harmony fixed dinner and told Marie about their pending appointment at a local rehab.

Marie said that she couldn't be happier.

That evening, Harmony prayed before she went to bed. She thanked God for her mother wanting help. She asked him to please let this be the rehab that would help save her mom's life.

That night, Marie couldn't sleep. That monkey was on her back. She tried to distract herself, but it kept bothering her. She often wondered why crack had a voice. She couldn't understand how or why that drug had so much control over her. She wanted so badly to be able to divorce it, but truth was, it was now a part of her. It told her to just get one last fix before she went to rehab. She said no, but that voice kept calling.

Harmony could hear her mother pacing back and forth. She got up to see what was wrong.

"Mom, are you all right?"

"No, baby, I'm not. Harmony, I just need to get high one last time."

Marie gave her daughter a look like a cornered cat, unsure of escape.

"Mom, you can't get high. I thought you wanted help."

Harmony felt her heart sink. She couldn't go through this again.

"I do, Harmony, but I just need to take the edge off," Marie said as she sat down on the bed and put her head in her hands.

Harmony walked over and sat next to her mother. Her eyes rested on the Bible that she had placed on the nightstand next to the bed. Harmony called on her newfound strength from the Lord.

She held her mother's hand and prayed. She prayed so long that it caused Marie to fall asleep. It was truly a blessing.

Marie spent forty-five days in rehab. Things were going well. She was looking great. She found a job and had some new sober friends.

Jake found out where she was and called often. He expressed to Harmony how he too wanted to change. He also wanted to be back with his wife. Marie was hesitant.

Harmony only had a one-bedroom apartment. The bathroom was located in the bedroom. She knew that she would be giving up her bedroom, but she allowed Jake to move in. She marveled at the fact that he was still in love with Marie, despite all they had gone through.

Jake moved in, and both were doing well. She found another place and gave them her apartment. She paid their first month's rent and deposit.

Harmony allowed work to be her focus. There was rarely any free time for herself or for God. Bishop Tate assured her that her walk with Christ wouldn't always be an easy one, so it was critical for her to stay in church and in prayer. However, she felt that she was strong enough in her faith to skip a couple of Sunday services. She just hadn't kept track of the months that had gone by.

She prayed as best she could, but half the time, she would be too exhausted to finish. She found herself falling asleep in the middle of the Lord's Prayer. She hoped that he understood that she was working hard because she didn't want to ever go back to selling her body.

Her plan was to save up enough money to be able to pay her rent for six months at a time. She also wanted to put some up for a rainy day. She already had a thousand saved. Two more would have her where she needed to be.

She made every effort to call Marie when she could. She told her that she was working like she was so they could have a brighter future. She really wanted to give her mother so much. She was proud of her for kicking her drug habit.

— ❧ 23 ❧ —

ONE DAY, HARMONY ACCIDENTALLY bumped into a man while leaving the bank

"Oh, excuse me," Harmony apologized.

"Apology accepted," said the man.

He caught her eye and smiled.

"Hello, sweetheart, my name is Flip. May I know yours?"

It had been almost a year since Harmony got saved. She had not dated or done any drugs since hearing those first words spoken to her in Bishop Tate's church. She often wondered if God intended for her to cut all communication because that's what she had done. However, saved life was starting to get a little boring for her. She wanted to meet new people.

"Yes," she replied. "My name is Harmony."

"Is there any way possible for me to get your number?"

There was a foreign accent to his voice that made Harmony curious.

"Where were you born?" she asked.

"I am Jamaican," Flip answered with a slight chuckle, smiling with confidence. "Now may I have your number? I would love to take you out."

Harmony allowed him to have her number.

That evening, Flip called and asked Harmony out. Despite her reservations, she agreed to meet him at Red Lobster for dinner. She chose the one on the west side of town, which was nowhere remotely close to where they were or even where she lived.

Harmony wanted to make him think that she lived on that side of town. She wouldn't lie if asked, but she knew that he would naturally assume that she did since she suggested that particular one. She had grown into a very cautious woman. Her philosophy was, "If I can't trust my own mother, who can I trust?"

At dinner, Flip was so courteous and attentive. He would help Harmony when she tried to get up from the table. He ordered many different appetizers so she could try them all. He made her order two meals so she could taste her two favorites at the same time. He was also a good listener. She told him about her walk with Christ. He told her about his.

She didn't know that Jamaicans were Christians. She judged them by the stories she heard. She thought they practiced voodoo— or, at least, the women did anyway. Flip showed her the Bible that he carried in his back pocket. He made it clear to her that he never left home without it.

The evening went well. She was comfortable with her new friend. She could see a friendship progressing.

What she couldn't see was a relationship beyond that. He just wasn't her type, not at all. Harmony was attracted to dark-skinned men with beautiful white teeth. Flip did have dark skin but yellow teeth, and a few of them were missing.

After their date, he would call daily and check up on her. She enjoyed the attention, but she knew that they could never be anything more than friends. He continued to call and often sent roses to her at work. The girls at the nursing home told her she was being crazy for putting them in her residents' rooms. She would tell the residents they were from their family members or friends. Some of them never had visitors. She just wanted them to feel loved.

She really didn't know how he was able to afford all that he was doing for her. She figured she would allow him to come over one evening so she could investigate.

He arrived at her door with a huge bouquet and a large gold box of chocolate.

"Hey, good looking! How are you this evening?"

She took the roses and chocolate and gave him a smile. "I'm doing great. And you?"

"Life is all too well, so I won't complain," Flip replied, with his ever-sunny Caribbean tone.

They sat down to a dinner of chicken, rice, and salad. Harmony had taken the trouble to light some candles and put a tablecloth on the table. While they were sharing some of the chocolates for dessert, Harmony decided it was time to ask.

"Flip, I would like to thank you for doing such wonderful things for me. The girls at work are jealous of all the attention you give me. They make comments about my leaving the roses with my residents. I even had one tell me I was self-centered because I was not thinking about your feelings. I leave the flowers for someone else to enjoy."

"Harmony, I do not think that is selfish at all. I sent those roses for you and the residents. I love that you share them."

Flip gave her a look that was as bright and warm as the candlelight on the table. He put another piece of chocolate on her plate and continued.

"Every day you're at work, I feel you are walking into a room that is filled with a reminder of me. Most of all, you're helping someone whose life may not be filled with color. I love sending different colors because that's how I view you. You are a woman of many colors. I appreciate that."

Harmony enjoyed his kind words, but she was curious about exactly what he was saying.

"What does that mean?"

"It means that you have been through so much, but yet you see the light behind all of it," he said. "You have a glow that only a spiritual person could see. You're the type of woman who puts others first. That is very attractive to me."

Harmony felt a warm spark in her heart. The way she saw herself reflected in Flip's eyes was how she had always wanted to be seen.

"Flip, thanks for seeing the positive in me."

She felt herself wanting to open up to him. But she caught herself before she got too carried away. There were still many unanswered questions about who Flip was.

"If you don't mind, I would like to know a little more about the mysterious man who knows more about me than I do him. I don't want you to think that I am not interested in your life because I am."

"Go ahead. Ask me whatever your heart desires." He gave her his widest smile again.

Harmony took a deep breath and then asked the question that had been weighing on her mind.

"We have talked openly about what it is I do for a living, but I don't know what it is that you do."

Flip seemed ready to answer. He leaned forward in his chair and folded his hands.

"Baby, as you know, I am Jamaican. Some of our beliefs aren't American beliefs. I am in a business that a lot of Americans don't agree with."

He paused and looked at Harmony. She stayed quiet, waiting to hear the whole story.

"In my country, marijuana is considered a form of medicine," he continued. "For us, it is a beautiful plant, grown from the earth. I have seen a lot of people with cancer feel better from it. I have also seen people who were considered blind be able to see."

The tone of his voice turned from romantic to more direct.

"I can't understand why America won't legalize it." He looked her in the eyes. "Baby, I sell weed. I sell a lot of it. I hope that it doesn't cause you to look at me any different."

Harmony's suspicions were confirmed. She had been wondering if this would be his answer. The path of this relationship was not yet clear to her, but she knew what her words to him had to be.

"I can't judge you," she said.

She had been through too much to judge the man in front of her. Her newfound dedication to the Lord provided her with the ability to forgive. But it also left her with a lot of questions about right and wrong.

Flip looked at her with the calmness of a man who has put everything he has on the table. He waited for her answer.

"You have left me with a lot to think about, Flip." Harmony was honest with him. "For now, it's late, and I have to get ready for work tomorrow. I don't know if I am ready for this relationship, but I will pray on it. I hope the Lord will give me some guidance."

"He always does," said Flip. "Sweet dreams, beautiful lady."

In bed that night, Harmony opened up her heart and prayed.

"What am I going to do, Lord? This man is a drug dealer. No, he doesn't sell crack, but he still is selling a drug that is illegal. I have been doing so good. I don't want to go back to being involved with those types of people."

She stared out into the dark and wondered, *God, is this a test? If so please, don't allow me to fail.*

$$\text{24}$$

FLIP CALLED AND ASKED if he could come and stay. Harmony had been staying in touch with him over the phone. She still was not sure if she wanted a relationship with Flip, but she enjoyed talking with him and told him she was still thinking things over.

She was a little surprised, but it made sense that he wanted to move. He had been roommates with a cousin of his, but his cousin was causing them a lot of heat. He was addicted to strippers and would bring a different one home every night.

He would also keep a lot of traffic in their home. Flip felt it was only a matter of time before the police raided them or someone robbed them.

He promised to pay all her bills since they weren't that much to him; in return, he just needed her couch to sleep on. Harmony felt six months was long enough to know what she needed to know about her friend. Plus, that extra rent money would help her cut back on the long, exhausting hours at work.

Flip had never made Harmony feel uncomfortable. He always had her best interest at heart. She knew that if she ever needed a place to stay, he would see to it that she had one. She knew that she couldn't tell him no.

"All that I ask is that you don't bring anybody to my house," Harmony said.

"No problem," Flip assured her. "I won't even tell my cousin. He runs his mouth too much."

Several months went by. Despite the constant compliments and advances, Harmony felt that things were going well. Flip had kept his end of the bargain by paying all the bills and not allowing anyone to know where they lived.

Harmony would go to work and come home and cook. If she didn't know any better, she would say that they were more than roommates. She made certain his clothes were clean and pressed. She would make certain he didn't run out of his deodorant or his favorite cologne.

They would go and rent movies from Blockbuster or go out to eat. He would buy her gifts all the time. She would also shop for him.

In a way, she was growing to care for their friendship the way two people do when they are in a romantic relationship, but she just couldn't allow herself to fall for him. She just was simply not attracted. Flip felt that they were making progress. Harmony wasn't seeing anyone at all. He decided to wait her out. He was certain she'd come around.

More time went by. Flip felt comfortable enough with Harmony to give her some big news about his business dealings. By now, Flip was up to kingpin status. He had a connect out of California who was giving him pounds of weed, cheap. He had decided to buy two hundred pounds and allow his connect to front him a hundred.

Flip knew that this was a win-win situation. He would make a profit off the supplier and a profit off the wholesale price. The only problem was how to move the product. He knew that it would be hard for him to get the shipment in by mail, and getting a moving van would also be a risk.

Harmony could see the worry on his face. Concerned, she asked if there was anything she could do.

"Baby, I am stuck," Flip confessed. "My man out of Cali gave me an offer I can't refuse. I just need to figure out how to get the stuff here. I can't have it sent. I can't go get it."

"Why not get somebody who drives a semitruck?" asked Harmony.

"Damn, baby, that's a good idea, but I don't know anybody who drives one."

Harmony had an idea.

"I might," she said. "Let me find my old phonebook."

One of her old clients named George owned a trucking company. She remembered that he was not always living life on the right side of the fence. He was in love with Harmony at one time and was even willing to leave his wife for her. Harmony knew if anybody could get the job done, it would be George.

She brought the number to Flip and told him her idea. After they went over the details of the fee, she placed the call.

"Well, hello, Handsome," Harmony said cheerfully.

"Harmony, is this you?" George's low voice answered on the other end.

"Yes," she said sweetly. "How are you?"

"I'm doing great now that I heard your voice," he replied.

"Thanks, George."

He cleared his throat on the other line. She heard the background noise go quiet and knew that he had moved to a more private location. After a few seconds, he spoke again.

"What can I do to make you change your mind about me?"

Harmony giggled flirtatiously and then gave a breathy sigh.

"George, you know that I can't break up your happy home."

"Well, is there anything that I can do for my dear friend?"

Harmony decided that would be her chance to ask him for a huge favor.

"Well," she smiled into the phone, "I might have an opportunity for you. Meet me at the City Center Mall so I can explain more."

"Anything for you, sweetness," he replied. "See you there in an hour."

"Great," she said. "Meet me at our old spot by the fountain."

Harmony got herself fixed up and told Flip she'd return shortly. On her ride downtown, she told herself what she was doing was right. The last time she had seen George, she was giving him her body. Times were different now. She didn't need to use her body, just her mind.

Wearing a black dress with matching heels, Harmony imagined herself to be a sexy, confident businesswoman as she walked through the mall on her way to meet George.

"Harmony, hi, sweetheart!" Mr. George stood up and took off his hat when he saw her approach the fountain.

"How are you, Mr. Stanford?" She leaned forward to give him a kiss on the cheek.

"I'm great now that I've had the honor of seeing my dear old friend," he said. "What can I do for you, Harmony? I can sense the urgency in your voice."

They sat down on the bench together to talk.

"George, I am going to be completely honest with you." Harmony turned to face him, resting her hand on his leg. "I have a connection out of California who has been helping me out. They gave my partner and me a deal that we can't refuse, but we have no way of transporting it. I know you used to help move some back in the day."

She knew George would have an idea what kind of shipment she was talking about.

"How much is it?" asked George.

"Three hundred pounds."

"Wow, that's almost a million dollars!" he yelled.

"That's a million plus on the street," Harmony confirmed. "I need you to use one of your trucks to get here."

"Sweetheart, if I were to get caught..." He blew out a deep breath and shook his head.

"You're not going to," she assured him. "My connect is dealing with someone who will load the truck. All you have to do is drive."

"I don't drive, you know that," said George.

"I need for you to drive. I can't trust anyone else but you." She looked him in the eye and prepared to deliver her sales pitch. "We will pay you eighteen thousand, plus gas mileage."

George's eyebrows went up. He watched the fountain and was quiet for a minute. Then he looked back at Harmony.

"When is this going down?

"If you leave out by Saturday morning…"

"I can get there Tuesday afternoon," he said.

"Good. So I take it that you'll do it?"

"Anything, for you."

"Thanks." Harmony stood up, and so did George. She gave him a tight hug.

"We'll meet you in the morning with all the details. Call me."

"I will," he promised. "Good to see you again, Harmony."

"Same to you."

Flip was a nervous wreck. He knew that he could trust Harmony, but he didn't know if he could trust the guy she had introduced him to. Being cautious was a trait with which Flip was born. He knew that he couldn't risk the shipment.

He decided that he and Harmony would follow the driver there and back. They would rent a car that had out-of-town plates to make it seem like they were on vacation. He hoped that Harmony would be up for the long trip.

Harmony was excited. She called into work and told them she needed some time off. She then went to visit her mother. She hadn't seen her as often as she had before. She had also slacked on going to church or even praying. She felt bad about that, but also she believed that God knew her heart.

Marie was doing great. She was working and had gained weight. She was really beautiful. Her chocolate skin looked like butter. It was creamy without a blemish. Her almond-shaped, brown eyes were framed by her still famously long eyelashes.

Marie told her to be careful on the trip. Harmony promised she would. Before leaving, Harmony gave her Mother two thousand to get herself some furniture.

Saturday morning came too soon. Harmony and Flip told George to meet them at 6:00 a.m. He was there a little earlier than that. She had mentioned to him that he would be transporting frozen meat that needed to be butchered. The weed would be stuffed inside the animals. They knew that once the inspector saw what was on the trailer, he would give George the okay. No one wanted to be in a freezer full of dead carcasses.

The trip there was a relaxing one; the trip back wasn't. Harmony was nervous every time they hit a checkpoint. Flip would caress her leg and tell her to just act normal. Once through, he'd distract her with conversation about their future.

"Baby, I am going to take care of you. All I ask is that you don't betray me."

"I will never do that to you."

"I got to be honest with you," Flip said. "I really don't trust too easy, but, Harmony, I trust you."

"I trust you too."

They talked about lots of things on the long drive. Flip told Harmony that she no longer had to work. Though she wasn't a lazy woman, she had always felt that a woman's role was in the house. She was starting to feel that maybe Flip was the man for her. Maybe she was hung up on appearances when she should really be focused on how she should be treated.

They all made it home from the mission safely. Harmony called Marie to let her know she was back. She unpacked Flip's and her belongings.

Flip called to check up on her and told her not to wait up. He said he had some work to do and to give him a call if she needed anything. She wanted so badly for that night to be their night, but she guessed that would have to wait.

Flip came home with ten pounds of weed. He had to unwrap plastic and dryer sheets from around it. It was never ending. He cut and pulled from one pound for about an hour it seemed.

Harmony didn't understand why he ordered her to wet towels and put them against the front door. She didn't realize how much of a scent ten pounds would give. She had to light incense throughout the apartment. She watched him weigh the weed with and without the covering. She saw him putting the weed in plastic ziplock bags. His phone was ringing off the hook. He didn't sit still long. He had to make one sale after another.

Money was flowing. Harmony was counting so much of it that her wrist would cramp up. She never thought she would see a hundred thousand in cash, but now she had. He made certain that he made love to her on top of it that night. As they lay together afterward, he promised her that to him, she was worth more.

He gave her money to put up for their future. He also made her put up money for her own savings.

Things had gotten to the point that they could no longer send money through the mail or drive it. The FBI did a bust a year earlier and found out that most of the transactions were done that way. Now they could only use Western Union. It was less of a risk to find someone with an ID and pay them a few bucks to send the money to the connect. If they were receiving a large amount of cash, they would take the risk and drive or fly to get it there sometimes.

Flip decided that the only choice he had was to fly the money there. He recruited two of his relatives to do the job. He had Harmony go and buy two girdles that would hold the money in place. He also told her to buy some duct tape.

Marcus and Brad came over to get ready for their flight. Harmony helped the men get into their bodysuits. They began to stuff themselves with money. Thirty thousand at first, and Flip and Harmony then had to wrap tape all around their chests and stomachs. They put their dress suits on and headed to the airport.

That was their routine for a year. Though he was making a lot of money, Flip knew that he couldn't spend it like he wanted to. He didn't want to rush and buy Harmony a home because that would raise suspicion. He also knew that he couldn't put the money in the bank.

He made Harmony take up her carpet and put the money under it. They then moved her bed so that it would cover the area. He took her to get a new car. Instead of buying it outright, Flip made her finance it. He wanted her to build her credit up. He also didn't want to give the dealership twenty thousand in cash for the Infiniti. He knew the Feds would be all over him.

"Harmony, I want to spoil you," Flip said. "There is nothing that I won't do for you. I just need you to always respect me."

"I promise that I will never disrespect you."

Though she wasn't in love with him at first, that soon changed. She looked at him and saw a man. She wanted so much to return all the love that he was giving to her. She knew that no gift she ever gave him would be enough. He showed her the kind of love that she only saw in the movies. He never wanted to take anything from her. He spoke to her like a man who loved his woman would.

"You're my star," he said. "As long as you shine, I am happy."

Flip loved her. He wanted to spend the rest of his life with her. He promised her that he wouldn't leave her ever. She was his soul. Harmony was so grateful to her man. Harmony catered to him like he was a king. She waited on him hand and foot.

She would cook three meals a day. She would make certain that he always had a clean house and clothes. After a long day of work, she would have his bathwater ran and would lotion and massage his head, hands, back, feet. She would also shine his boots. Whatever he needed from her, she'd do.

※ 25 ※

WORD GOT OUT ABOUT the Jamaican who was eating. People even knew that Harmony was his girl. The black Infiniti gave it away. They knew no average girl would be driving one. Flip was getting word that people were talking about robbing him. He knew that they wouldn't get much because he didn't carry much.

No one knew where his stash was, not even Harmony who was his right arm. It wasn't that he didn't trust her; it was just the less she knew, the less she would be held accountable. He came home and told her that they would have to switch things up. He needed for her to find them another place, preferably on a different side of town. He went to her front office and paid for her to break her lease.

They packed and made arrangements for movers to take their stuff to a storage place outside Columbus. He made hotel reservations for them. He told Harmony to put the car in another storage place.

Harmony was afraid for him. She knew that the streets didn't play fair. She also knew that Jamaicans didn't play fair. Though Flip was humble and laid low, she also knew that he wasn't someone to be played with.

She hoped that all that was just talk that would eventually die down. She was enjoying life and the fruits of their labor, and now that was being threatened. They had to live in a hotel for two weeks before she got the keys to their new apartment. Flip had made it clear that they had to move in a complex so no one could ever know which apartment they were going to.

He said he wouldn't even feel comfortable if her mother knew where they stayed. Harmony would have to visit her and make sure not to tell her what side of town they stayed on. Harmony hated to keep something like that from her mother, but she knew that Flip knew best.

Flip's cousin Brad was the only person who was allowed to know their address. Brad wasn't one of Harmony's favorite people. She couldn't understand why Flip trusted him. She had stopped long ago.

She hated when he came around because he always made passes at her. He told her that Flip wasn't going to be the one to always call the shots. She felt that he wanted to be in Flip's shoes.

"Star, he just looks up to me," Flip assured her that he was harmless. "His crush on you is understandable. You got it going on."

Harmony was treating herself well, and it showed. Flip always made sure she had what she needed; and she made sure to keep her hair freshly done, her nails manicured and polished, and she always sparkled with beautiful jewelry. Reynoldsburg was her favorite destination. That suburb had any store she ever wanted. She shopped all day long.

Flip continued to work. He made it clear that he wanted her to enroll in school. He told her that he wanted her to have something to fall back on, just in case something was to ever happen to him. She promised she would. She had to trade her car in for something less noticeable. She settled on a Maximum.

Marie was proud of her daughter. Harmony had proved her wrong. For years, she thought that Harmony would be the one to follow in her footsteps. She thought that at least one of her children would have to end up like her—at least, that was what she had been told.

Though the two had shared similar experiences, they were completely different, and Marie thanked God for that. She told Harmony that she was happy that she was now able to have a relationship with her children. She hated that she had missed so much of their lives and vowed to make up for it anyway she could.

She and Jake worked hard to save their marriage as well as to stay sober. They went to AA meetings every other day.

Harmony was proud of her mother. She didn't mind helping her with bills or putting pocket change in her purse. Harmony liked to treat Marie to a good time. She would take her on shopping sprees. They would go to lunch or to a movie. They would even go to plays.

The one thing they couldn't do was go to the place where Harmony lay her head down. Marie understood.

"Girl, he's trying to protect you," Marie said to her daughter.

Harmony didn't feel so bad since she said it that way.

Valentine's Day was right around the corner. Flip went and made reservations for them at the Homewood Suites. He had also gone to Roberts Jewelers and bought a two-carat engagement ring. He was ready to take their relationship to the next level. He hoped that she would say yes when he popped the question.

He hid the ring in the trunk under the spare tire. He had to take a trip to Arizona, but he told Harmony that when he returned, "It will be all about me and you, Star."

The trip he was taking would be their first time apart.

"I'm going to miss you, but I know this absence will only make our love grow stronger," he told Harmony.

Behind the scenes, he had decided to go and ask Marie and Jake for their permission. They both agreed and were happy. They liked Flip a lot. They knew that he had Harmony's best interest at heart. They also knew how much she loved him.

He made them promise not to say a word. He informed them that he would propose on Valentine's Day. Marie couldn't keep from crying. Her daughter was about to be engaged!

Harmony made certain that she packed all that Flip would need for his trip. She was sad that he had to take the trip alone. She wanted to go with him, but he assured her that his connect out of Arizona didn't want him to bring anybody, not even Brad.

From the sound of it, Brad wasn't too happy either. He felt that he was Flip's right-hand man and there was no reason why he should be left behind. Flip told him that it was not his choice at all. He wouldn't dare take a trip like that without him. For some reason, the Arizona connect didn't trust anybody but Flip. Whomever Flip dealt with was Flip's business; he just didn't want to meet them.

Flip promised to call Harmony when he got there. He did just that. They talked on the phone the entire time he was gone. He would tell her how much he loved and missed her. She would cry and tell him how much she needed him.

"Baby, not as much as I need you," Flip would say.

To Harmony, the four days seemed like an eternity. She tossed and turned all night.

Finally, it was time for Flip to return home. Harmony woke up bright and early. She had to get things ready for her man. She and Marie had gone out and bought him clothes and a dog. He was fond of English bulldogs. She knew that would make his day.

Harmony decorated the house to welcome him home. She knew that he would be home at eleven that morning. She found the skimpiest teddy she could find. Victoria's Secret had a pink one that she knew would drive him wild. She had offered to pick him up, but he said Brad was going to do it.

He called right before his plane was to board. He told her to pack her overnight bag. She made certain to pack them two outfits each. She didn't know where they might be going, but she trusted him. She couldn't wait to see him home soon.

One o'clock came, and she still hadn't heard from Flip. His plane was over two hours late. She called him and Brad again and again. There was no answer.

She paced back and forth. She knew something wasn't right. Time came and went, and all her calls went unanswered. She didn't know who to call. There was no question—she was never going to call the police. No one would know where Flip was anyway, except the connect. She spent the rest of the evening pacing around the apartment. There was nothing she could to do but cry and pray. Finally, she fell asleep on the couch, waiting.

Sunday morning, she was awakened by a knock at the door. It was Brad.

Immediately she felt her heart start to race, but she didn't want Brad to see how shaken she was.

"Brad, where is he?" Harmony said.

"Baby girl, I hate to tell you this, but when I went to the airport, he wasn't there," Brad said. "I even tried to see if he had boarded the plane, and they said he hadn't. I waited there for three hours to see whether he had taken another flight, but he didn't."

Brad was acting very suspicious. Harmony wondered what he was really there for. She told herself that she would play things off as best she could.

"How come you didn't answer my calls?"

"Because I couldn't hear the phone ringing at the airport. I think his connect in Arizona set him up," he said, opening his eyes wide.

"Why? Why would he do that? He needs Flip," said Harmony.

"That fool don't need him. He got foot soldiers out here."

Harmony swore that Brad was talking about himself in third person. She couldn't help but wonder why he was talking about Flip in the past tense, but she held her tongue. Marie didn't give birth to a fool. She knew to ask the fewest questions.

She could tell that Brad knew more than what he was telling. She also knew that Flip indeed boarded that plane. She had the phone call to prove it.

"Harmony, I'm going to need to know where that stash is."

"What stash?" said Harmony.

"Come on now, Harmony. I know he told you where the stash is."

"No he didn't!" she yelled defiantly.

"Baby girl, he told me he let you in on everything."

Harmony had to think quick on her feet while she repeated past conversations between Flip and her in her mind. She could vividly remember him saying, *"No one knows about this but you, me and, God, so keep it that way."*

"He told me the less I knew, the better," she said.

Brad gripped the edge of the door and seemed like he didn't know what to do next. He looked away and then back at Harmony.

"All right, if you hear anything, call me."

Harmony was sure something happened to Flip. Shortly after Brad left, she called her mother and told her everything. Marie agreed with her suspicions. She told Harmony to hope for the best but prepare for the worst.

Brad's versions of events played over and over in her mind, *"Because I couldn't hear it ringing at the airport. I think his connect in Arizona set him up."*

Bullshit, she thought to herself.

Harmony knew that it would only be a matter of time before Brad came back. She also knew that it would be too much of a risk for her to stay there. She started packing what she could. She then pushed and pulled until she could get under their bed.

She needed to get underneath the carpet. That's where they had the stash strategically placed. She packed the stacks in suitcases, then carried the bags to his truck. She knew that she was taking a risk moving it in daylight, but she knew trying to move it at night posed a risk far greater.

By the time she finished, she was exhausted. She still hadn't heard from Flip. She couldn't bear the thought that she never would. With the bags safely stored in the truck, she drove to a hotel for the night. Exhausted, Harmony collapsed onto the bed and turned on the television.

The eleven o'clock news came on with a news flash.

"A man was found shot to death in an alley. He appeared to have been in a struggle. An eye witness has come forward…"

Harmony knew that was Flip. She knew that had to be him. How else could she explain him not being there? He loved her and would have never left her, other than death.

She was right. The news announced that the victim's wallet had been found at the scene.

"Franklin Jones was the name of the victim," the news anchor shared.

Harmony lost all hope. She cried so hard. She sat in that hotel room in desperation. Memories flashed through her mind. She thought about moments they had together, sharing their hopes and dreams and making plans for their future. She thought about her life without him. She knew only God could sustain her.

Marie called her, but she wouldn't answer—she couldn't answer. She just wanted to take time to get her thoughts together.

Harmony knew that she would have to call Ms. Jones and tell her the news.

"Hello, Ms. Jones?"

"Harmony, is this you?"

"Yes, it's me." Harmony could barely get out the words.

"What's wrong, honey?"

"Ms. Jones, he's gone."

There was a long pause. Harmony felt like her heart had disappeared from her chest. She listened to the silence on the other end of the line and stared out the window of her hotel room at nothing.

"Harmony, please, tell me all you know, baby," finally, Ms. Jones spoke.

Harmony told Ms. Jones everything. Ms. Jones told Harmony that she too knew that Brad was behind it. He had always been envious of her son. She had told Flip that she didn't trust her nephew. She told him not to let Brad know where his money was. Harmony told her that he took her advice.

Ms. Jones told Harmony to take that money and start a new life away from Columbus. She told her that she was going to have his body sent back to Jamaica and that she would have his funeral recorded for her. She didn't trust Brad and knew that he would go downtown to identify the body. She didn't want Harmony nowhere near there.

She told Harmony to change her number and to call her just as soon as she got a new one. Harmony told Flip's mother that she had more than enough money and that she wanted to send her some.

"No, baby, I'm fine," said Ms. Jones. "My son would have wanted his wife to be taken care of."

"His wife? We weren't married, Ms. Jones."

"He wanted you to be. He was going to propose to you yesterday. Harmony, the ring is under the spare tire."

Harmony couldn't believe what she was hearing. She was supposed to be engaged right now.

"How could God allow Brad to get away with this?" she wailed.

"Surely he wouldn't," Ms. Jones assured her. "Flip has people still. Brad will get his due. Honey, please remember my son and think about all the good times you shared together. And please, stay in prayer."

"I will," Harmony promised.

Harmony finally called Marie. Her mother had already seen the terrible news earlier. She told Harmony how sorry she was and that she was there if she needed her.

She told her mother she would have to leave the city. Marie told her that would be a good idea. Harmony was glad she had never allowed Brad to meet her mother. She never revealed where she lived. Before hanging up, she promised Marie that she would keep in contact with her.

Harmony cried and wailed until the tears wouldn't fall.

Finally, she was exhausted. It was now time to decide how to act. She decided to go to the truck and get her ring. After digging it out, she couldn't believe what she had laid her eyes on. The platinum band sparkled, with a solid big diamond in the center and baguettes on each side. It was simply beautiful.

She slipped the ring on her finger and spoke out into the darkness, "Yes, I will marry you, Flip."

She went back to her room and counted the money. She couldn't believe that it was three hundred thousand. She thanked Flip for taking care of her, even after his death. She promised herself and him that she would get far away from Columbus.

The next day, she got up, packed her things, and left.

She longed to have a simple life, a life far from what she was used to. She wanted to go to school for nursing. She could see herself walking across that stage receiving her degree and Flip smiling down at her.

For hours she drove. She played all the songs they liked to listen to. She cried one moment and laughed the next. She thought about how Brad thought she would give him the money that was at the house. She wondered if they would ever find all the weed that Flip stashed. Also, she wondered if Brad had help when he tried to rob Flip and if so, then from who?

She knew that it wasn't right to hate, but she hated him. She hoped that he would get his.

Harmony settled on a small town in Virginia called Petersburg. It was home to several military bases. She didn't know how life here would be, but she was willing to try it.

Hell, what did she have to lose?